The Dreadful Future of Blossom Culp

Also by Richard Peck

Novels for Young People
Don't Look and It Won't Hurt
Dreamland Lake
Through a Brief Darkness
Representing Super Doll
The Ghost Belonged to Me
Ghosts I Have Been
Are You in the House Alone?
Father Figure
Secrets of the Shopping Mall
Close Enough to Touch

Novels for Adults
Amanda/Miranda
New York Time
This Family of Women

Picture Books
Monster Night at Grandma's House
(ILLUSTRATED BY DON FREEMAN)

Nonfiction Anthologies
Edge of Awareness
(COEDITED WITH NED E. HOOPES)
Leap into Reality

Verse Anthologies
Sounds and Silences
Mindscapes
Pictures That Storm Inside My Head

RICHARD PECK

THE DREADFUL FUTURE OF BLOSSOM CULP

DELACORTE PRESS/NEW YORK

Published by
Delacorte Press
1 Dag Hammarskjold Plaza
New York, N.Y. 10017

First printing

Library of Congress Cataloging in Publication Data

Peck, Richard.
The Dreadful Future of Blossom Culp.
Summary: Blossom, not the most popular member of her
freshman class in 1914, travels ahead seventy years, and
returns in time to make Halloween a memorable night for
her classmates and teachers.
[1. Space and time—Fiction. 2. School stories]
I. Title.
PZ7.P338Dq   1983   [Fic]   83–5165
ISBN 0–385–29300–3

For Patsy and Ron Perritt, in friendship

The Dreadful Future of Blossom Culp

1

UNLESS YOU NEVER GOT OUT OF GRADE SCHOOL, you'll have noticed how life keeps making you start over.

In the year of 1914 my class went from being eighth graders at Horace Mann School to being freshmen at Bluff City High School, which is just across the road. Being the youngest and newcomers over there, we were all regarded as lower than a snake's belly. I don't know who sets such rules. My name is Blossom Culp, and I live by rules of my own.

I've been looked down on before, plenty, so turning into a freshman didn't hit me as hard as some I could mention. Letty Shambaugh liked to die of shame. She's lived all her fourteen-plus years with her nose in the air, her paw being the owner of the Select Dry Goods Company.

On the other hand, the last time my paw showed his face in Bluff City, my mama run him out of town. Above her head Mama waved an empty blended whiskey bottle, the blended whiskey itself being in Paw. Though she could outrun him sober, she kept just at his heels to the city limits.

I only mention this to show the difference between me and Letty Shambaugh. Her mama can
keep her paw in line with one hand while running
the Daughters of the American Revolution with the
other.

Letty lives in the lap of luxury in a large all-brick
house on Fairview Avenue, famous far and wide for
its good taste. My mama and me occupy a two-room
dwelling by the streetcar tracks just behind the
Armsworths' barn. Though Mama and me have
made improvements on it, every election year some
candidate or other promises the voters he'll have our
place demolished in the interest of progress.

Never mind. The world is full of Letty Shambaughs, and this includes the high school. But there
is only one Blossom Culp, and I am her.

That's more or less what Miss Mae Spaulding said
to me on the last day of school. Miss Spaulding is
both eighth-grade teacher and principal of Horace
Mann, being not only a very learned woman but
well organized.

When Miss Spaulding called me into her office,
Letty Shambaugh and all her little club of girls
pointed their fingers at me and hooted.

Letty, looking shapeless in her shell-pink graduation dress with a big corsage stuck to her shoulder, twitched her elbows and said, "I expect Miss
Spaulding has bad news for Blossom. I have an idea
Blossom is to be held back."

All the girls in her club, which is called the Sunny

Thoughts and Busy Fingers Sisterhood, agreed with her, like they're supposed to.

I didn't dignify this charge with a reply. There was no earthly reason I'd be held back to repeat eighth grade. Nobody would. It was clear that Miss Spaulding had had enough of all of us, which is more or less what she said to me.

If you've ever been summoned to a principal's office, you know the feeling. Decorating Miss Spaulding's wall are a bust of the poet Longfellow, a portrait of President Woodrow Wilson, and a well-worn paddle. I'd been in there before, and there's nothing homelike about it.

Though Miss Spaulding has no more figure than a runner bean, she makes up for it with posture. But on that day she was somewhat bent, as teachers get toward the end of a school year.

It had been a busy afternoon. We'd had the handing out of diplomas, several speeches, and the traditional maypole dance. Then we said the Pledge of Allegiance one last time and called it a day.

It had all tired Miss Spaulding worse than regular routine, and I hadn't seen much point to it myself. She settled into her desk chair and seemed to wilt.

"Well, Blossom, we have lived to see this graduation day."

"Yes, ma'am."

"You and I have had our little differences over the years, have we not?"

I nodded, recalling several.

"Without checking the records," she said, "I believe I saw you first in this office in fourth grade."

"Yes, ma'am. That was the year me and my mama moved up here from Sikeston. And naming no names, a bunch of girls dragged me into the rest room and pretty nearly took me apart."

Miss Spaulding sighed. "I am afraid, Blossom, it was something you must have said that . . . excited their curiosity."

"Oh, well, shoot," I said. "Any little thing will set them off."

"Then along about sixth grade," she continued, "there was that blue racer snake that Maisie Markham found in her lunch bucket. The poor child actually put her hand on that thing, thinking it was liverwurst sausage. You will recall how the experience affected her digestion."

I remembered clearly. Anybody would. "She's gained all that weight back since and then some."

"The culprit, however, has never been brought to justice."

"It wasn't me," I said.

"It wasn't *I*," Miss Spaulding said.

"I never thought it was."

She sighed deeper. "What is past is past, I suppose. But I wonder if much progress has been made. I refer to the maypole dance today."

She was closing in on me fast. But this is America, so I hoped to have a chance to defend myself.

"I am not referring to your dress, Blossom. Never think it."

Letty Shambaugh had decreed that all the girls should wear shell-pink, made up of yardage purchased at her paw's Select Dry Goods store. I was hanged if I'd go along with that. I wore my gray princess dress, which there is still some wear in. On my chest I planted my spelling medal. I'm a champion speller, which comes in handy in the writing of this true account.

I even perked up my outfit with a new purple sash, which was as far as I'd go. There was nothing to be done about my hair, which kinks in this weather.

"I am referring to the maypole dance itself," Miss Spaulding said, "after all those rehearsals that went so well. How long did we rehearse our dance, Blossom?"

"Every dadburned night for a week," says I, "weaving them ribbons around that pole, with Letty Shambaugh bossing us all like she was—"

"It would have been a lovely spectacle," Miss Spaulding said, "so graceful with all the ribbons making pretty patterns. But it was not to be, was it?"

"Fate moves in mysterious ways," I said.

"Who, Blossom, do you suppose went to all the work of digging around the maypole in the dead of last night and undermined its foundations? Who so unbalanced the pole that one sharp tug on a ribbon would bring the whole pole crashing down, barely missing Ione Williams's head and grazing Letty's corsage? Who, for that matter, gave a ribbon the sharp tug? I grant you, it made all the boys laugh, if that was the intention."

"Anything will make a boy laugh," I said. It was a regular scandal how the finger of blame always pointed my way when any little thing went wrong.

"But we must let bygones be bygones." Miss Spaulding sighed. She'd waved me into a chair, and there I sat, swinging my legs, waiting for her to come to her main point, which she always does.

"Next September, Blossom, you will be across the road at the high school. This is a first-rate opportunity, if you will but take it, to make a fresh start with a clean slate. You will find high school very different. It would be fortunate if high school did not find you so . . . different. Do you follow me?"

I thought I did. "Lay low and keep my nose clean?"

Miss Spaulding looked pained. "In so many words, yes. Blossom, you are growing up and beginning to become a young . . . lady. Anytime now your . . . form may begin to fill out."

She looked down at her own form, which never has, and cleared her throat. "You will develop . . . new interests, such as your personal appearance and daintier habits."

I wiped my nose on my sleeve and wished she'd come to her point without going all around Robin Hood's barn. She can be very plainspoken if she tries.

"In short, Blossom, I think it would be better for you and the community at large if you put some of your old habits to rest. There are better ways of getting attention than dabbling in the . . . occult."

"If you mean my Second Sight," I said, "it's no prank, like the snake in Maisie's lunch or the maypole—whoever pulled them stunts. It's a Gift, and it's in the blood. I get it from my mama, who is seven-eighths Gypsy. Mama could take a squint at your tea leaves, Miss Spaulding, and read your whole future like a book."

"That won't be necessary," she replied. "I know my future."

"You do?"

She nodded. "Once you are across the road at the high school, my future will be smooth sailing. I look forward to some much deserved peace and quiet."

"Mama could give you a closer reading than that," I said. "Mama could pinpoint the hour of your death to a minute!"

Miss Spaulding flinched. "Blossom, there are people who do not want the hour of their deaths . . . pinpointed. There are people who think all this . . . spiritualism is hogwash."

"They're ignorant."

"Nevertheless"—Miss Spaulding straightened several small items on her desk—"it's high time you learned how to get along in *this* world without worrying about . . . other locations."

"When the fit comes over me and I get my Vibrations, seems like I don't have much say in the matter. You remember yourself, Miss Spaulding, that time right here in this office when I had one of my spells. I was here and elsewhere all at once. You sat right there and watched my spirit wander back in time until I found myself aboard the steamship *Titanic* just when it took its fatal—"

"Please, Blossom." Miss Spaulding put out her hand like a crossing guard. "You need not refresh my memory. The event is still vivid in my mind. I have given your . . . experiences long thought, and I have come to the only possible conclusion, a scientific conclusion."

She paused. "You will have heard the term 'puberty,' Blossom?"

The term rang a bell with me, but I couldn't exactly put my finger on it. Miss Spaulding's face had gone beet-red. She cleared her throat a number of times, rapid-fire.

"Puberty is that time of life when a young girl begins to become . . . an older girl. It is a time of considerable . . . upheaval to body and brain alike. I have concluded that your . . . psychic episodes were purely a temporary condition. Do you comprehend my meaning?"

"I can see ghosts, too," I told her.

Miss Spaulding wilted more till her chin was on her chest. You never saw a tireder woman. Trying to help her out, I said, "You mean, I was going through a stage and now I'm beginning to outgrow it?"

She perked up. "Precisely, Blossom! Put your past behind you and all your . . . exploits. Over at the high school they like team players. I'm sure you can settle down and be one if you put your mind to it."

"I guess I could try," I said.

"Try, and you will succeed!" Miss Spaulding sang out. "Do not be tempted, Blossom. If you begin to . . . Vibrate, or whatever it is you do, or if some thoughtless classmate goads you into showing off, turn a deaf ear!"

She heaved herself up from her desk. "Mind over matter, Blossom. Let that be the motto for your future!"

*

Throughout the summer of 1914 I thought over Miss Spaulding's advice. I supposed it was possible that I was outgrowing my Second Sight. Mama always says my Powers are puny compared to hers, though she's the jealous type. I even thought it might be just as well if I was more like other people. I was about half-willing to lay my Powers to rest.

But that's where Fate stepped in. I was to learn it isn't possible to turn away from my talents. A Gift is a curse if you don't put it to work.

As a freshman at Bluff City High School I was often to recall with a wry smile how Miss Spaulding had warned me to look to my future. For I was to set foot into a future world beyond all Miss Spaulding's scientific conclusions, even beyond the imaginings of any person now living.

I was to see the Dreadful Future firsthand for myself, and as plain as the nose on your face.

2

ON A WARM SEPTEMBER MORNING my route to high school took me around the Armsworth family barn and across their property. My mama economizes on breakfasts, kicking me out of the house early, so on my way I'm always greeted by the smell of frying bacon coming from the Armsworth mansion.

Alexander Armsworth, a kid of my acquaintance, lives there. He can't help but know me since we're near neighbors. However, Alexander managed to avoid me all that summer like I had the typhoid fever.

Him and me have reason to be friends, though a boy rarely listens to reason. We're the only two people in Bluff City with the Second Sight, except for my mama. I get my Gift from her. Where Alexander gets his is anybody's guess.

Seems like all he does is deny he has it. One time he saw a ghost right there in the loft of the Armsworth barn. Locally that outbuilding is still known as the Ghost Barn because of this famous happening. But it took wild horses to drag a confession out of Alexander.

Let him catch one glimpse of a haunt or some poor restless soul in search of a decent grave, and he turns tail. A boy hates to show fear worse than poison, and when it comes to the Spirit World, Alexander Armsworth is scared of his own shadow. He is girl-shy, too, or at least shy of me.

But he is not bad-looking. I lingered along that morning under the bay window of the Armsworth dining room, hearing the clink of knife and fork and Alexander's mama whining. But there was no reason to linger, though I kicked a certain amount of gravel. If Alexander spied me from the bay window, he'd take to the cellar till I was off the place. He treats me worse than a ghost.

I slowed again when the high school hove into view. As Bluff City is an up-and-coming place with better than twenty-two hundred inhabitants, they have a first-rate high school.

It was larger than I remembered, and the entire student body was milling around outside, many of them as big as grown-ups. Nearly all the female sex was in long skirts. The boys parted their hair in the middle and gummed it down with grease. Everybody was trying to look like everybody else with much success.

Some that I took to be juniors and seniors were arriving in autos—roadsters and touring cars and such—and the country ones were coming in by the wagonload. The football team showed off by tackling each other on the field out back. It was a sight.

Everybody seemed well acquainted with everybody else, calling out greetings. Though I'm used to going it alone, I wouldn't have minded knowing someone to call out a greeting to. But the only familiar faces I saw were Letty Shambaugh and her club of girls. They'd congregated around Letty for mutual protection under a shade tree. She seemed to be getting them organized. I don't look for friendship or even common decency from Letty, so I was willing to pass them by.

But Letty hollered out, "You there, Blossom Culp! I want a word with you." At that her whole club turned my way.

Ione Williams was there, and Harriet Hochhuth and the Beasley twins, Tess and Bess, who are identical, and Maisie Markham, who stands out a mile.

Letty has the sweetest little face you ever saw until you come to her mouth, which is mean. She bustled up and began to speak. Then her eyes popped when she saw the spelling medal I wore depending from my front.

"Well, if that doesn't about take the cake!" she exclaimed. "Wearing that old grade school spelling medal to high school!"

"Did you ever?" said several of her club.

"They are not going to be interested in your so-called past achievements here at the high school," Letty continued. "Take my advice and throw that thing away."

I made a silent vow right then to wear that spelling medal on my chest until it fell off.

"But never mind about that," Letty said. "What I want to say to you is this, Blossom. You will find here at the high school they have such a thing as school spirit. The freshman class must pull together, and as Miss Spaulding used to say, 'A chain is only as strong as its weakest link.' "

Letty left no doubt as to who the weakest link was, and all her club looked right at me.

"We don't have any intention in this world of being dragged down or embarrassed to death by you, Blossom. Let this be a warning." Her eyes narrowed to slits.

"Is that a fact," I remarked.

She patted her hair bow. "You cannot help your background, Blossom, or do much about your looks. But I hope in my heart you won't make a jackass of us all by telling tall tales and poking your nose into other people's business and claiming you are some kind of a witch or whatever, which are three of your bad habits."

There are times in life when it's better to remain silent and let your fists do the talking. I was winding up to knock the socks off Letty Shambaugh when I caught a glimpse of Alexander Armsworth in the distance, which distracted me.

He was wandering into the schoolyard in a new belted knicker suit with his eyes peeled for two high school cronies of his, Bub Timmons and Champ Ferguson.

Then from within the schoolhouse a bell rang, the first of many. Everybody ganged toward the entrance. Alexander was claimed by Bub and Champ, and Letty surged ahead with all her club. I was left to face high school alone, keeping Alexander Armsworth in the corner of my eye.

I suppose high school is educational, though very little of it is to my taste. The teachers can teach only one subject, so you spend half the day traipsing from one classroom to the next, herded along like hogs in a chute.

To keep us freshmen in our place, we all had to wear what they call beanies, which are little orange and black skullcaps with the number 18 on them, as we are to be the graduating class of 1918. I had to anchor my beanie on my unruly hair with a hatpin.

As headgear they are not flattering, though Letty wore hers like a crown of jewels. On Maisie Markham's big head, the beanie looked like a covered button. But if you turned up without one, some sophomore had the privilege of wiping the floor with you.

Our days began with a thing they call homeroom. Here attendance is taken and announcements are made. All the freshmen are stuck in the same homeroom, so it was no better than being in Horace Mann School. In the first week we had class elections. Letty was made president of the class, and Alexander was made vice-president. My name didn't come up.

Our homeroom teacher was an ancient person, name of Miss Blankenship. We returned to her later each day for English literature, where she was driving us with a whip through a play called *Hamlet*. Every day she put a new quotation from this play on the blackboard, such as:

SOMETHING IS ROTTEN IN THE STATE OF DENMARK
Act I

which was written out in her quavering hand. Until Miss Blankenship, I hadn't known that a woman can go bald, too. But she wasn't blind. One false step and she nailed you.

Though I could put up with most of high school, I nearly drew the line at what they call Girls' Gym. I get all the exercise I need, and I'm not in the habit of taking off my clothes in public. Still, we all had to take it except for Maisie Markham, who was excused on the grounds of weight.

I'd expected the gym teacher to be a big, beefy woman, like a heavyweight wrestler in bloomers. But here I was proved wrong.

Her name was Miss Fuller, and she was more willowy than muscular. She wore a bandeau of flowered silk tight across her forehead and artistic drapings in several colors hanging down over her bloomers. Satin ribbons that attached to her gym shoes crisscrossed to the knee over her cotton stockings. She had a wan face and sad spaniel eyes with a suspicion of rouge dotting both her prominent cheekbones.

Under her direction, we ran relays and swung Indian clubs, but she favored what she called Artistic Expression. She'd crank up an Edison Victrola and play a song called "Pale Hands I Love Beside the Shalimar." To this accompaniment we were to turn ourselves into fields of waving wheat or sometimes flowers sprouting and putting out foliage.

She was a great one for graceful movement, and I'd often fall down, as I found it hard to maneuver in bloomers and rubber shoes. I wouldn't have minded it much except for the locker room. Here we had to strip down and shower together in a big galvanized metal enclosure.

Every now and then me and Mama drag a washtub in from the porch at home and have a bath before the fire. But we take turns.

In Girls' Gym we all had to splash around under the spigots together. This was not natural to me, particularly as Letty Shambaugh took it for an opportunity to make remarks about my person.

Her person, which I glimpsed through the steam and soapsuds, was pink and dimpled all over. I could only hope this bathing business wouldn't continue on into cold weather, which is not good for your health.

From Girls' Gym we went daily to the study of history. It was taught by a new teacher, name of Mr. Ambrose Lacy. Many of the sillier girls had crushes on him. Because Letty Shambaugh sat across the aisle from me, I happened to notice she'd written Mr. Lacy's name on her notebook cover, encircled it with a heart, and lettered in the following poem:

If you love me as I love you,
No knife can cut our love in two.

Sickening though this was, Mr. Lacy took it in his stride, seeming to have a long history of being admired. He was a handsome man and knew it, with regular features and a cleft in his chin. His hair was yellow and wavy, and all his neckties and pocket handkerchiefs matched. As high school teachers go, he was about average, but he struck so many vain poses that I personally thought he'd have done better on the stage.

He was fond of the sound of his own voice. One time early in the semester he clasped his hands in the small of his back and proclaimed: "Rome is dead, and the once-great British Empire is on its knees. But Bluff City is in her prime! Where else on earth do the tracks of the Wabash Railroad and the Illinois Central cross, creating prosperity and a top-notch daily wage for those willing to work?

"Boys and girls, we had better search the history of Bluff City to learn why we're sitting so pretty. What is history but mankind's record where we look for guidance? We search the past for wisdom because the future is the Great Unknown!"

"I'm not so sure about that," I said, speaking out before I thought.

Mr. Lacy looked down at me, startled. He'd been as cranked up as Miss Fuller's Victrola before my interruption. "You aren't?"

"Well, no," I said. "An aunt of mine foresaw the

future, so it wasn't the Great Unknown to her. Here awhile back she had a vision of the San Francisco earthquake a week ahead of the actual event."

Across the aisle Letty Shambaugh threw herself onto her desktop and began drumming it with her little fists. "Oh, no. Blossom's going to tell more lies about her trashy family. I could just die. Somebody stop her." Et cetera.

But Mr. Lacy paid her no heed. He hadn't noticed me before, but now he did. "Did your aunt make this—ah—prophecy known?"

"Shoot, yes," I explained. "She was living right there in San Francisco at the time, in a rooming house on Mission Street. She preached the earthquake's coming from the street corners and notified all the newspapers."

"I see," said Mr. Lacy, staring at me like a cat had spoken.

"It didn't do her any good, though, as it turned out."

Letty moaned. "Oh, don't let Blossom finish the story. Her endings are always simply awful. Somebody stuff something in her mouth." Et cetera.

"Nobody likes hearing bad news," I said, "so my aunt was widely ignored. She began to lose faith and to disbelieve her Powers, and that led to a regular tragedy."

"It did?" said Mr. Lacy. The whole classroom had gone quiet except for Letty moaning.

I nodded. "My aunt failed to save herself. Her

vision foretold that the entire south end of the city would collapse into its own cellars. But on the night before the great quake she just went to bed like anybody else. Of course, when it struck at dawn and she was throwed across her room and felt the floor give under her, she was proved right.

"But it was too late to get out. Down she crashed and ended up pinned under half a house. Alive though she was, she'd have been left to rot except that one of her arms was poked through the wreckage and stretched exposed on the sidewalk."

Mr. Lacy shuddered, but all the boys were attentive. Ahead of me, Alexander was listening. He wouldn't turn around, but I saw how red his ears were getting.

"There my aunt was," I said, "like a rat in a trap all day with only her hand and arm free out there on the public pavement."

I dropped my voice as I came to the terrible part of this true story. "On that hand my aunt wore a diamond ring. Imagine her horror and dismay when some looter came along on the sidewalk outside and all but trod on her helpless hand. Then he looked down and saw it.

"This looter fellow hunkered down and took hold of her hand, which my aunt tried to jerk away. Then he saw it wasn't a dismembered limb or lifeless. By then he'd noticed the diamond sparkling on one of her fingers.

"He took her hand in his rough grasp and commenced to twist at her ring, determined to take it from her. But it was a tight fit and wouldn't work loose.

"Well, sir, the looter rubbed my aunt's finger raw, but he couldn't pull that doggoned diamond ring over her knuckle. All this time she was screaming from under the house, unheeded."

I fell silent then to give everybody time to picture this awful scene and to figure out what was coming next if they had any imagination.

"Then my ill-fated aunt knew the worst when her hand was raised to the looter's stubbled face. She felt the hot wetness and sharp teeth when his mouth closed over her ring finger."

The classroom was tomb-silent. Mr. Lacy, who is naturally pale, went paler. "You don't mean," he began, "that—"

"You bet your boots," I said. "The damnable looter chewed my aunt's finger off and bit the bone in two. Then he made away with her ring. The fire department didn't dig her out till nightfall. They never located her diamond ring, though her finger was found in a gutter nearby just where the looter had spat it out."

The room remained hushed except for the pounding sound of Maisie Markham's feet as she galloped to the door with both her hands clamped over her mouth. Maisie doesn't have the stomach for a good story.

3

I SAT BACK PRETTY WELL SATISFIED at this true story of my nine-fingered aunt.

Besides, it was history, being about the San Francisco earthquake, and this was history class. But across the aisle Letty was clutching her forehead. Up ahead Alexander sat slouched in his seat, his ears burning with embarrassment. A person knows when her efforts to contribute aren't appreciated. I got no better from Mr. Lacy.

He swallowed heavily and said, "Blossom, since you're responsible for this upset, you'd better skin on down to Miss Fuller's locker room and see that Maisie is all right. The child may need to stretch out on the cot down there until she's better."

"I'll need a pass," I said, reminding him of one of the many rules around this place.

"Just go, Blossom," he barked, so I went, making a dignified exit.

Any moment of freedom in a school day is worth its weight in gold, so I took my sweet time getting down to the locker room on my errand of mercy.

Since high school teachers don't work a full day, they have such a thing as a free period. Miss Fuller was having hers when I finally sauntered into her office at one end of the lockers.

She was at her desk busy with paper work. But Maisie was nowhere in sight, and she's hard to miss. When I explained that I'd been sent down on her behalf, Miss Fuller recounted how Maisie had lost her lunch on the way here but had recovered enough to be sent home.

"She has a weak stomach," I remarked. "She stuffs her face with candy the livelong day—licorice and suchlike."

"A very unhealthy habit," Miss Fuller noted.

"And nasty," I added.

As I had no place to be, I lingered at Miss Fuller's desk, noticing that she was extra wan-looking today. Behind the horn-rimmed reading spectacles, her magnified eyes were more soulful than usual. Though she'd seemed intent upon her paper work, her mind was drifting. This is the sort of thing I can often tell about people, don't ask me how.

I expected to be sent on my way, but Miss Fuller's thoughts were off gathering wool. I thought of taking a peek at her gradebook, but who cares about a gym grade? Then my eyes fell upon a fatal document.

It was a note on the desk. There was a page of writing that ended with numerous X's, representing kisses. I knew that handwriting even upside down.

My eyes popped, but I kept a poker face. It was a letter from Mr. Lacy.

Miss Fuller seemed to notice me again. "What class did Maisie get sick in?" When I told her, she only said, "Ah." But her hand fluttered up to the back of her neck. "Ambrose—Mr. Lacy is quite a good teacher, I believe?"

So-so, I nearly said, but I was on my guard now. "He is right good," I remarked, "and many of the girls are sweet on him."

"Indeed?" she said.

Naming no names, I quoted to her the poem Letty Shambaugh had written to Mr. Lacy on her notebook cover. I hoped to share a good laugh with Miss Fuller, but I was in for another surprise.

" 'No knife can cut our love in two,' " she echoed. "That is a real beautiful sentiment."

It was about the worst corn-fed sentiment I'd ever run up against. But something was dawning on me fast. Love had come to Miss Fuller. She had it bad for Mr. Lacy, and being a gym teacher, she didn't know a good poem from drivel.

She sighed and returned to her work, but she was watching me on the sly. Since I often do the same, I can tell when it's being done to me. Miss Fuller's hand skated over the papers on her desk, concealing Mr. Lacy's note and picking up another page.

She stroked the artistic knot of hair that rode high above her bandeau. "Speaking of poetry," she remarked, "how does this strike you?"

She read aloud in a mournful voice like the coo of a mating dove:

> "Thoughts are bluebirds high above,
> Winging toward you with my love;
> Soaring over oak and pine,
> They bring the news that I am thine."

I like to have gagged. This poem was more sickening than Letty's. Miss Fuller had no doubt cribbed it off a two-cent valentine.

"What do you think?" she asked, and waited for a reply.

My head whirled. Not only was Miss Fuller stuck on Mr. Lacy, but she was writing slop to him like a young girl. It shook my faith in grown-ups.

"I have heard worse," I said cautiously, though I never had.

Miss Fuller sighed again and plucked at the tails of her bandeau. "Don't be kind," she sighed. "My poor words are unworthy. For me, Artistic Expression is limited to the dance. With poetry, I seem to strike out."

She'd get no argument from me on that score.

"I don't suppose you know any . . . suitable poetry, Blossom?"

I could see the woman was desperate, so I racked my brain. Then suitable poetry came to me. It was Miss Blankenship's daily words from *Hamlet*, which had seeped into my head.

"How about this?" I said.

"Doubt thou the stars are fire;
　　Doubt that the sun doth move;
　　Doubt truth to be a liar;
　　But never doubt I love."

Miss Fuller blinked at me from behind her horn-rims. Her hand stole up to her long cheek. "That has a nice ring to it," she said. "Did you write it?"

"No, but Shakespeare did," I explained, "in *Hamlet*, Act Two."

"Nevertheless," she said, "it seems to hit the nail right on the head." She pushed paper and an ink pen across the desk at me. "I'll be much obliged if you'd just copy out those words. I would like them for . . . my scrapbook of Beautiful Thoughts."

She grew shifty-eyed then as people will when they're lying.

The bell rang just as I finished my copy work. I was ready to scoot, but Miss Fuller looked up in a dreamy way, saying, "You are a strange child, Blossom, and not a promising physical specimen. Still, you are somehow sympathetic."

"Many thanks," I told her, as these were the first halfway civil words I'd heard in high school. Then I cut out.

The schoolyard was emptying when I stepped out into the afternoon sunshine. There, at the foot of the steps, stubbing his toe in the earth, was Alexander Armsworth. Reminding myself how Miss Fuller could make a fool of herself over the male sex, I meant to breeze past him in case he had no greeting for me. But he did.

"Well, Blossom, you've put your foot in it again with that tall tale about your so-called aunt getting her ring finger gnawed off."

With so much on my mind, I'd nearly forgotten history class until this rude reminder. Alexander smoothed the front of his argyle sweater and expanded his chest to its limit.

"Now that we're in high school," he said, "we're not kids who'll swallow everything we're told."

"Is that a fact?" I retorted. His voice had changed some more over the summer, and he clearly liked the sound of it. I lit into him.

"Alexander, I've had it up to here with lectures. You're sounding more like Letty Shambaugh every minute, and it'll be a cold day in you-know-where when I need advice from either one of you."

I felt my face heat up, though I'd meant to keep calm. A person can take only so much.

"I'm only speaking for your own good, Blossom. And of course, on behalf of the freshman class." He pointed to his beanie. Being provoked, I scanned the ground for a rock big enough to lay across the side of his head. But there's never one when you need it.

"Some friend you turned out to be, Alexander," I said, more in sorrow than in anger. "Here I am just coming out of Miss Fuller's locker room with some real interesting news I might be willing to share. But all you can do is carp and complain. I suppose you were hanging around just to put me in my place."

Alexander cast his eyes to the sky. "Don't flatter yourself, Blossom. I'm hanging around because we're going to have a meeting of freshman class officers."

"You and Letty are getting too thick to stir," I remarked.

Alexander spoke then of what he called "the entire slate of officers." Letty had appointed Harriet Hochhuth secretary, Ione Williams treasurer, and Tess and Bess Beasley sergeants at arms.

"Trust Letty to make officers out of her whole club," I said. "And what business do you have to conduct anyhow?"

Alexander drew himself up importantly. "One item of business is the Halloween Festival, when each class holds a fund-raising event. Us officers have got to come up with a crackerjack event for Halloween night to show the entire school there are no flies on the freshman class."

"Is that a fact?" I replied, as this was the first I'd heard of the so-called Halloween Festival. "It sounds to me like the school's trying to keep us busy on Halloween night so certain parties I could name won't get up to mischief and outright vandalism."

"That kind of Halloweening is kid stuff, Blossom." Alexander spoke in his deepest voice.

"Then you've come a long way from last Halloween, when you and Bub Timmons and Champ Ferguson and Les Dawson came to considerable grief when you tried to turn over Old Man Leverette's privy."

Alexander's ears went pink. He pushed right past me up the steps to his freshman officers' meeting. But at the top he turned to fire a parting shot.

"And, Blossom," he said, "take my advice and stop wearing that old grade school spelling medal. Nobody gives a hoot in high school." Then he vanished.

There I stood, without a friend in the world and eight months to go in the school year. Though I can generally manage to keep my sunny side up, my spirits were low on that October afternoon.

But it is always darkest before the dawn. I was to find a friend sooner than I knew, and in quite an unexpected place.

4

WHETHER IT'S DUE TO MY SECOND SIGHT OR NOT,
I've always been drawn to people—even the living
—who are lonely or troubled in their thoughts. It
seems to be my fate. Possibly Miss Fuller pining for
love of Mr. Lacy at her desk in the locker room is
an example. A better example than her cropped up
in the following week.

For reasons of his own, Mr. Lacy formed the
habit of sending me off on various errands during
history class. As this gave me freedom and a relief
from history, it suited us both.

One afternoon I was killing time after I'd deliv-
ered the attendance slip to the main office. As is my
habit, I dropped into the girls' rest room down in the
cellar of the school.

Mama and me don't have running water piped in
at home, so the sight of all that white tile and rush-
ing water at your beck and call is a comfort. More-
over, the conveniences are all in little cubbyholes
with doors on them. I believe people deserve their
privacy, especially me.

The girls' rest room is strictly modern with rolls of paper where you'd expect to find pages from the Sears, Roebuck catalogue. I was sitting at my ease in one of the cubbyholes that afternoon when something came over me that seemed supernatural. Though I didn't Vibrate, my flesh crawled as I sensed I wasn't alone.

With the thought came a low sob from the next cubbyhole. Glancing down, I saw under the half wall between us a foot planted there in a broken boot. Another sob followed the first. When I heard paper tearing from the roll, I figured my neighbor was of the living. Still, you never know.

Settling my skirts, I stole out to investigate, but my squeaking door gave me away. The next door over was yanked open from within, and there I stood, staring straight inside at a girl still sitting.

She had a pinched face and a slack jaw. Slumped there with her skirttails hitched up, she was blowing her nose with a square of the paper they provide. Her nappy old flannel jacket and a feed sack skirt made me a regular fashion plate by contrast. From her general condition I took her to be one of the kids in from the country. Her hair was arranged roughly into pigtails, and there was more than mud on her boots.

It's not my way to stand around chatting to people in these circumstances. But the girl gazed up at me with eyes as sad as Miss Fuller's, set in a face far sadder.

"You didn't see me," she said in a country drawl. "Bear that in mind."

"If I wasn't to see you, why did you open your door?"

"I get lonesome," she whined, sniffing a red nose. "I reckon I'd have opened up even if you'd been one of them teachers. It's a sight how lonesome you can get in a big, busy place like Bluff City."

It was neither big nor busy there in her cubbyhole, but I let that pass.

"You a freshman?" I asked, just making small talk.

"I reckon," she replied.

"Then where's your beanie?" I pointed to my own, bristling with a hatpin on my head.

"Is that what them things mean?" she said. "I wondered."

Country children are slow to catch on to our ways, but this example was slower than most. I began to have suspicions.

"Say, listen, if you're a freshman, how come you aren't in Miss Blankenship's homeroom?"

"Who?" The girl drew back. "What?"

I had her cornered, and she saw that, so I changed my tack. "My name's Blossom Culp. What's yours?"

She didn't like giving out her name. But finally she said, "Daisy-Rae," looking like she might try to climb her wall.

"Pleased to meet you, Daisy-Rae. Why don't you come on out of . . . there? This isn't any way to carry on a conversation." I strolled away to the sinks to give her time to pull herself together.

"Well, all right," came her voice from the cubbyhole, "but just for a minute."

The plumbing at the high school is first-rate, but I'd never run across anybody so fond of it before. My suspicions deepened as they often do. Something was definitely rotten in the state of Denmark.

A chain was pulled from within. Water flushed, and Daisy-Rae edged out. She was a tall and gawky type, putting me in the mind of a wild turkey. Her pigtails were tied up with binder twine, and her elbows were out of her flannel shirt sleeves.

"You in from the country?"

"How'd you know?" said Daisy-Rae.

*

That's how I found a new friend. Unless you're slower than I thought, you'll have figured out what I saw at once. Daisy-Rae was a stowaway here at Bluff City High School. She'd never signed herself up on the rollbook, and she'd never darkened the homeroom door. Daisy-Rae had been down here in a cubbyhole of the girls' rest room since Labor Day, sitting her life away.

I confronted her with the facts of her case just to clear the air.

She turned a ghastly green. "How do you know so much?" She glanced toward the door, but it was too late to run.

"Oh, I have my ways," I said. "For one thing, I'm

Gifted with the Second Sight. I can see the Unseen and the Living Dead, which is about what you are, hanging out down here day in and day out."

"Oh," said Daisy-Rae, kind of goggle-eyed, "I thought we just run into one another by accident."

"Well, in this case we did," I admitted. "But what I can't figure is this: How come you don't go to class like everybody else?"

Daisy-Rae rammed one big toe against the other. She was one awkward girl. "Well, I *meant* to," she said. "I come to school that first day, but all them faces in that big schoolyard was just a blur. I says to myself, *Daisy-Rae, you're nothin' but a girl from the backwoods and the hollers. A place like this could chew you up and spit you out.*"

I nodded in sympathy, knowing the feeling.

"Then a bell rung, like they do," Daisy-Rae went on, "and everybody ganged into the schoolhouse. When I got inside, nobody said boo to me, and I didn't know which way to turn. I come across this indoor outhouse, so I just went in one of them little horse stalls, banged the door shut, and flopped down."

"Well, I never," I declared. "And you been here ever since!"

"I go home at night," Daisy-Rae said. "You can leave after they ring that bell the sixteenth time."

And I thought I'd heard everything.

"Of course, this place fills up with girls at lunch and in them short spaces between the bells."

"Them—those short spaces between the bells is

when we're going from one class to another," I explained.

"Is that right?" says Daisy-Rae. "That's interesting."

"What do you do when the other girls come in here?"

"I just pop out of my stall and mill around with them at the sinks. None of these girls notice me. Seems like they can't focus on anybody they don't already know."

That's about the size of it.

"At lunch I go out in the schoolyard and climb that shade tree out there."

"I never noticed you," I said.

"Well, that's the point, ain't it? They wouldn't know one country kid from another anyhow. The teachers ain't no different."

Bad though her grammar is, Daisy-Rae rattled on, being starved for company. I didn't mind, as I found her story interesting. She was rawboned as a new colt, but she had her wits about her. I admire that.

"Beats me why you go to all the work of coming to school at all. Your paw and maw make you?"

Daisy-Rae flapped a bony hand in the air. "Aw, naw," she said. "Paw's dead, and Maw's up in Michigan, pickin' fruit. I come to town on account of Roderick. He's my little brother. That one-room school out in the country wasn't doin' him no good. So I brought him in here and signed him up at the Horace Mann School across the road. I thought I'd

come over to the high school and pick up some education for myself till I thought better of it."

"Your brother . . . Roderick . . . was he too smart
for a country school?"

Daisy-Rae pondered, scratching her head with a
long finger.

"To tell you the truth, they couldn't do nothin'
with him there. He's medium simple."

"How's he doing at Horace Mann?"

"Oh, right well," she said. "In town it seems like
they take a long time to catch up with you."

She had a point there. I could have named her
several numskulls of my acquaintance who got
passed from grade to grade eventually.

"Roderick don't mind it," Daisy-Rae said. "Of
course, he'd just as soon be one place as another."

This world is full of wonders. Daisy-Rae was one,
and I had no doubt that Roderick was another. "If
you'll take my advice," I told her, "you'll turn yourself in and start going to classes. I grant you, it's like
a stretch in jail, but at least it's not solitary confine-
ment." I made a meaningful gesture to her stall.

"Well, I wasn't lookin' for advice exactly," Daisy-
Rae said in a thoughtful way. Then fear entered
her watery eyes. "You wouldn't turn me in, would
you?"

"Who me?" I replied. "A friend wouldn't do that,
and you can count me as a friend."

My words seemed to work magic. Daisy-Rae was
pitifully snaggle-toothed, but her smile shone with a
rare beauty then. It was a cautious smile to begin

with. Then she beamed at me, and her eyes brimmed
with tears.

The bell rang, rattling the window grates.

"That's old number sixteen," Daisy-Rae noted.
"Another day, another dollar, as the sayin' goes. I
reckon we can all go on home now."

5

Just when I'd been feeling extra-friendless, now I had me a Secret Pal. In the weeks that followed, I'd nip down to the rest room after my errands and pass the time of day with Daisy-Rae. We both looked forward to it. Once in a while, during biology or *Hamlet* or the shower room, I even envied Daisy-Rae her quiet life.

Still, her situation worried me. "I know you got to wait around till your brother gets out of school every day," I said to her, "but why don't you get out and walk around the town or something?"

She waved this well-meant suggestion away. "I'm nothin' but a country girl, and I'd get lost in a big place like Bluff City. Besides, I'll need a warm spot like this, come winter."

"You're a truant, you know," I informed her.

"I thought a truant was one who don't come to school," she replied. "I come to school."

She had me there.

Out in the schoolyard at lunch, she stayed up her tree. But she could talk the gold out of your teeth when we were on our own down in the rest room. In worldly ways she was backward. But there were no flies on her when it came to noticing things.

"That towheaded boy in the fancy sweater," she said to me one time, "you got a soft spot for him?"

I like to have dropped my teeth. "If you mean Alexander Armsworth," I said, "I don't know what you're talking about."

Daisy-Rae smirked. "I seen the way you look at him out there in the yard. He's standoffish, though, ain't he?"

"Alexander goes his way, and I go mine," I said, somewhat prissy. But you don't stay on your high horse long around Daisy-Rae.

"That Alexander," she remarked, "he's runnin' in bad company."

There was more truth than poetry to that observation. "You mean those two big galoots, Bub Timmons and Champ Ferguson," I said. "Alexander's a very well-brought-up boy, and he's trying to live it down. I've told him myself he ought to stay clear of Bub and Champ. Bub's spent five semesters in the sophomore year, and Champ's old enough to get married."

"Don't I know it," Daisy-Rae said, smirking again. I suspected she knew more than she was letting on.

"What do you know?" says I.

She reached down under her skirts and scratched at a flea bite through a hole in her stocking. "When nobody notices you're there, you hear things. Besides, Roderick and me, we live out just past Leverette's Woods. We cut through on our way home. You know that swimmin' hole out there with the big rope hangin' down?"

"I heard tell of it," I said.

"Well, them three—that Bub and Champ and yore Alexander—they mosey out there about every afternoon these warm days to swim. That's where they do their big talkin' and smokin' and makin' plans for Halloween. It's a sight. Me and Roderick, we spy on 'em."

"Smoking?" says I. "If Alexander's mama gets wind of him smoking, she'll wear him out. And as to Halloween, what are you talking about, Daisy-Rae? Alexander's on the committee for the Halloween Festival. He's left Halloween pranks and stunts behind him, to hear him tell it."

Again Daisy-Rae smirked.

*

That's how I happened to pay a visit out to Leverette's Woods myself one mild October afternoon, guided there by Daisy-Rae and her little brother, Roderick. Whatever Alexander was up to, I meant to get to the bottom of it.

Old Man Leverette once owned all that territory out past the streetcar trestle over Snake Creek. He owned the woods that bear his name, with a well-known Lovers' Lane winding through it and the swimming hole. He also once occupied a large frame farmhouse just beyond the woods, now going to rack and ruin. Come to find out, Daisy-Rae and her brother occupied a chicken coop behind the old abandoned Leverette farmhouse.

Old Man Leverette himself has retired into Bluff City. However, since he's a lover of peace and quiet, he'd have done better to keep to the countryside.

I met Daisy-Rae under the shade tree after school. She knew how to blend in with the crowd. I never saw her coming till she was right there beside me.

She wasn't easy in her mind till we'd crossed the road to where her brother, Roderick, sat waiting on the steps of Horace Mann School. He was a pathetic little gnome of about nine, and there was no doubt that him and Daisy-Rae were blood kin. Like her, he was slack-jawed, with a face far older than the rest of him.

As his only garment, he wore a small pair of bib overalls. His bare shoulders had no more meat on them than a coat hanger. He shambled toward us. His posture was bad, and since he was clutching his middle, I figured he had the bellyache.

But Daisy-Rae, being a big sister, summed up the situation. "Now what have you got?" she inquired, taking him by an ear and giving him a good shake.

Roderick's teeth rattled, but he said nothing.

"Come on." Daisy-Rae turned his ear inside out. "Let's see what it is this time." She reached down inside the bib of his overalls and felt around in there. Presently she drew up a long tail with a gray mouse struggling at the end of it.

I'm not nervous of vermin, but the idea of carrying around a live mouse with those scratchy little claws down the front of your overalls gave me the willies. Daisy-Rae swung the mouse by the tail over her head and let fly with it. The mouse lit running.

"I swan," she said to me, "I have to shake him down every blessed day, and you wouldn't credit what I find on him."

She got a good grip on his hand, and off the three of us strolled, out past the sidewalks and into open country.

"You can call me Blossom," I said, just to put Roderick at his ease.

But Daisy-Rae said, "He won't call you nothin'. He don't have a lot to say."

When we got out past the trestle bridge and onto dirt road, I noticed that Daisy-Rae was less gawky. Even Roderick, who had a tendency to drool, drooled less. When we reached the wire fence around Leverette's Woods, they both vaulted right over it with easy grace. I had to take it in stages.

In the woods they followed a faint trail like a pair of Indian scouts. Not knowing the territory, I tended to crash through the underbrush. At length Daisy-Rae drew me up short, whispering, "When we get to the swimmin' hole, we'll skin up that big elm tree. I have an idee we won't have long to wait." Roderick had already slipped on ahead of us, quiet as a . . . mouse.

The swimming hole's a quarter of a mile back into Leverette's Woods. When we came to the elm tree beside it, I'd have given up if I hadn't been set on getting the goods on Alexander and his chums. I'm no squirrel for climbing trees. I gazed up the elm's tall trunk. There high in the foliage was Roderick's face, peering down already like a somewhat dim-witted owl.

Daisy-Rae boosted me from behind, but I'll never know how I shinnied up the ten feet to the first branch. I was about to give out when Roderick's small, grimy hand shot out of the greenery and guided me onto a branch. There I settled while Daisy-Rae swarmed up behind me and eased onto a nearby limb.

Roderick settled on a perch of his own above us. They were both as natural up a tree as a pair of bats. I was giddy looking down until I got my bearings. Through the leaves I had a fine view of the swimming hole and a patch of tall grass directly below.

"Hark at that," Daisy-Rae murmured before I heard them coming. She had ears on her like a librarian. "Sit real still, and don't swing yore legs nor nothin', and they'll never know."

Not a minute later, following the sound of small bushes being tramped down, Bub Timmons and Champ Ferguson stepped out of the woods right under me. With them was Alexander.

"Whooeee," remarks Bub, "won't that water feel good."

"Last one in," says Champ, "sucks eggs."

Alexander said nothing but threw himself in the weeds and commenced wrenching his shoes off. Durned if they didn't all three start shucking off their clothes. Somehow I hadn't thought this far. The grass was soon littered with shoes and shirts and Alexander's argyle sweater and boys' union-suit underwear. Quicker than tongue can tell, Bub, Champ, and Alexander were all naked as jaybirds.

"Well, I never," I whispered to Daisy-Rae.

"You have now," Daisy-Rae whispered back.

They were soon all neck-deep in the water, but not before I had an eyeful. They splashed and ducked one another as boys will, playing the fool. Then Alexander heaved out of the pond on the far side and pulled himself up a tree where the big rope swing hung down.

What a sight Alexander was, clambering up that tree as naked as the day he was born. He looked for all the world like a plucked chicken. Then he edged out on the branch where the rope was.

Pounding his chest with both hands like Tarzan of the Apes, he roars out in his deepest voice:

"O, WHAT A ROGUE AND
PEASANT SLAVE AM I!"

which made Bub and Champ in the water hoot and catcall.

"What kind of talk would that be?" Daisy-Rae whispered to me. I explained it was just Alexander showing off with lines from Miss Blankenship's *Hamlet*, which, of course, meant nothing to Daisy-Rae.

Nearly overbalancing, Alexander dragged up the knot end of the rope and swung out over the swimming hole. He swung right at me, his legs high and wide. I sat real still, taking in the view before he turned loose and hit the water.

By and by the three of them dragged themselves out to dry off in the last rays of the sun. They flopped down in the weeds beneath us and commenced to brag, describing what kind of tattoos they'd all get once they were grown and free of Bluff City.

Bub declared he was going to have a big heart tattooed on his shoulder with a place left blank for lettering in the name of his sweetheart when he was ready to settle down. Champ favored a Chinese dragon with a tail wrapping his arm from elbow to wrist. Trying to keep up, Alexander said he wanted the American eagle tattooed completely across his chest. But Champ remarked that on Alexander's chest there wouldn't hardly be room for a wren.

They all laughed like hyenas and wrestled around in the weeds till Bub pulled out a tobacco pouch and papers and rolled three cigarettes. The air was soon foul and blue from their puffing. Alexander had a job to keep his lighted. He was going green around the gills, though the rest of him was white as chalk. He barely got the thing smoked, and then if he didn't say, "I'll have me another of those coffin nails, Bub, if you don't mind."

I rolled my eyes at Daisy-Rae, and she rolled hers back from her branch.

Halloween soon came up in their conversation. I

was all ears to hear Alexander say, "I won't be available on Halloween night itself, what with the Halloween Festival that I am in charge of." It was something to hear how important he could make himself without a stitch on.

Bub and Champ pointed out that it was fair and square to Halloween any night around the end of October. Indeed, to do all the damage they proposed, it would take them most of a month. And since boys rarely come up with any new ideas, their plot turned upon Old Man Leverette. They're out to get him every year.

I found myself leaning far forward to hear their disgusting plan to plague Old Man Leverette. They could hardly get it discussed for rolling around in the weeds, helpless with laughter and anticipation. It was a nastier plan than turning over his privy, and I about had to give them some credit for originality.

I had no time for anything else because disaster struck right about then. I heard what seemed the crack of a nearby rifle. Daisy-Rae gave out with a little gasp, and above me Roderick drew up his bare feet.

Then the world went topsy-turvy. The rifle crack was, in fact, my branch breaking. It held my weight for an instant more. Then suddenly I was dropping through the air in a blizzard of whipping leaves, following my big branch to the ground.

I had only time to think that if I wasn't killed, I might finish off anybody I lit on. There were startled yelps from the boys below as the sky seemed to fall on them. I believe they began to crawl different ways, but they didn't get far.

I rode that thing like a bucking bronco, leaving Daisy-Rae and Roderick far above me. It seemed to take forever before I crashed to earth, jarring my eyeteeth. Where there'd been weeds and naked boys, now there was a jungle of leafy branches and quivering twigs. I nestled, somewhat stunned, in the midst of it.

Very near me I heard bad language from the surprised Bub. Champ muttered, too, and then I heard Alexander's voice.

"Oh, no, lightning must have struck. Where is my underwear? I can't go home like this, and I'd better be going." Et cetera.

I had the sense to keep quiet. Let them all think lightning had struck, and it would be far better for me. I began to crawl backward along the limb, trying to slip away unnoticed while the boys untangled themselves.

Chancing a look up in the tree, I saw Daisy-Rae's boots still dangling from her branch and all but invisible. Roderick remained up there, too, looking down at me, almost interested. Then I stole away in a low crouch, bruised all over.

I'd have made a clean getaway, but my toe snagged in a root, and I went sprawling. Glancing back, I saw Alexander's head popping up, wearing a sort of wreath of elm leaves. He could see me, too, unless he was dazed. I had no intention of hanging around to find out. Boys are modest to a fault. I lit out like a jackrabbit.

Through the woods I sprinted until I got a stitch in my side and slowed to a walk. There was nothing to hear but birdsong. The evening shadows were growing long on the ground. Getting my breath back, I began to slip along, practicing Daisy-Rae's and Roderick's quiet way in the woods. With a pair of moccasins in place of my boots, I wouldn't have made a bad Indian.

Having had enough excitement for one day, I took my time finding a way out of the woods. But there was more to come.

Sharpening my senses, I seemed to hear murmuring somewhere through the brush ahead. I thought of cooing doves before the sound became a man's baritone voice.

Bending double, I made my careful way along behind a screen of elderberry bushes. More like a frontierswoman with every stealthy step, I sensed open country ahead of me. The man's voice droned on, nearer now. One false step would betray me, so I worked along extra-careful.

Still, I almost blundered onto them. Ahead of me were open fields and Old Man Leverette's abandoned farmhouse outlined against the sunset. Nearer, just within the woods, was the Lovers' Lane, winding its way. Beside the gate into the Leverette pasture a pair of lovers stood beneath a weeping willow tree.

Luck was with me. I was still a good five yards

away with an elderberry bush between me and them. I hunkered down quick, barely breathing. In that position I was to suffer several nasty shocks.

The lovers were locked in embrace. I couldn't see the lady, she being in the arms of a broad-shouldered swain in a blue serge suit. He seemed to be reciting poetry to her. He turned his profile aside and proclaimed these well-known lines:

> "Doubt thou the stars are fire;
>   Doubt that the sun doth move;
>   Doubt truth to be a liar;
>   But never doubt I love."

It was Mr. Lacy. The sunset played across his yellow hair. While he paused for a moment of dramatic silence, the lady emitted sighs. I was all ears.

"Oh, how perfectly lovely, Ambrose," says the lady in a familiar voice. "It is like you to choose lines from Shakespeare, knowing how fond I am of all his works."

Surely my ears deceived me. But no. Mr. Lacy bowed to cover the lady's hand with kisses, and I saw her face plain. It was Miss Mae Spaulding, principal and eighth-grade teacher of Horace Mann School.

My heart was in my throat at horror and dismay to find my old grade school principal in the embrace of Mr. Lacy. You're never too late for love, I suppose, but what of Miss Fuller, the deceived gym teacher?

While Miss Fuller was languishing in her locker room, here her beloved stood, quoting the same Shakespeare I'd provided her with to another woman. You talk about a snake in the grass.

They fell to kissing again, Miss Spaulding firmly under his spell. I'd thought she had better sense, but then I'd only seen her during a school day. The spectacles she always wears on a chain had fallen off her nose and were swinging free. Her hair was escaping from its bun, and Mr. Lacy was all over her. Before I could recover from this shock, I got another one, quite a lot worse.

Staring intently through the bush at these so-called lovers, I failed to protect my backside. Maybe I heard a twig snap behind me, maybe not.

A hand closed like a claw on my shoulder. Another thorny hand, scarcely human, clapped over my mouth. My breath was cut off, and my heart hollered. Pinned though I was behind the elderberry bush, I wrenched my head around.

I was staring up into a fearful face with eyes sharp as black diamonds boring into mine. Then I was scared for sure. There aren't two faces like that anywhere in North America. It was my mama.

6

ANY SCENE WITH MAMA IN IT is always painful to recall. Though I could have walked, she dragged me clear back to town by the scruff of the neck. Over her humped shoulder was a sack of hickory nuts. Mama is a fortune-teller by trade, but in the fall we add to our income by nut gathering. We also do a certain amount of gardening, often in other people's gardens.

On our homeward trip we paused once for her to cut a switch off a bush for my legs. Mama isn't up-to-date on child raising and is liable to whup the tar out of me over any little matter.

At home she flung me into a chair and eased the sack onto the floor, saying, "Ooph'll larn youoph to fool arounph in theph timber, youoph little—"

"Mama," I said, "put your teeth in if you're going to talk." I can understand her anyhow but hoped to distract her. She won't wear her teeth much, a good artificial pair, and will leave them around most any-place. Luck wasn't with me, as they were right there on the table between a pack of playing cards and her crystal ball. She popped them in, which fills out her face no end, and turned on me.

"Now listen, Mama," I said, talking fast. "I only went out to the woods to learn what a bunch of boys were going to pull on Halloween. You know yourself what damage they can do if some responsible person such as myself doesn't put a stop to it."

Mama's snaky eyes narrowed. She thrust her terrible face closer to mine, and her earrings swayed. They were a pair of gambler's dice hanging from her lobes, which is an example of Mama's taste in jewelry. I talked faster.

"I didn't set out to spy on Mr. Lacy, my history teacher, who's two-timing Miss Fuller, the gym teacher with Miss Mae—"

"Shut up," Mama remarked, taking up the switch. Her mean gaze fell on my legs.

"It was an accident, pure and simple. I just chanced onto that Lovers' Lane, where—"

"You was creepin' up on that house. I caught you at it." Mama lashed the air with her switch, testing it. I tried not to notice.

"What house?" I inquired.

Thwack went the switch on the tabletop with a dreadful sound. "The old Leverette place, don't play goody-goody with me."

It's remarkable how plain Mama can speak with her teeth in. They grinned at me, but she didn't.

"The old Leverette place?" I echoed. Mama seemed to be off on one of her tangents.

Thwack on the table again. "You heard me. You

don't go near that place. I tell you one time, you listen." *Thwack* yet again.

"I don't have any business in Old Man Leverette's tumbledown place."

"You can say that agin," Mama mocked, but she'd turned loose of the switch. It rested on the table as a stern reminder. There was something going on in Mama's mind.

"You keep clear of that place," she advised, "or I'll slap you to sleep."

"Why, Mama?"

She grunted, somehow pleased. "I knowed you hadn't figured it out. Ain't I told you time and agin your Powers is puny compared to mine? I won't have you dabblin' in things you can't handle. I got my reputation to consider."

It began to dawn on me. "You mean the place is haunted?"

"I know what I know." Her teeth clacked in some satisfaction. "You don't know nothin'."

Nobody likes to be talked down to that way, especially by a mother. I tried to reason the situation out. "It couldn't be haunted by Old Man Leverette. He's alive and kicking right here in Bluff City."

Though she was still looming over me, Mama drew out a pouch of Bull Durham chewing tobacco from the black folds of her shroud. She pulled off a plug and popped it into her mouth. While she jawed it down to size, I gave the matter more thought.

"Was there a halo about the place?" I asked her. Mama can occasionally tell if a place is haunted if she sees a mystical halo arching over its roof. It's one of her better ways.

"If you had any Powers whatsoever," she responded rudely, "you'd know that for yourself."

At least she seemed to forget the switch. A plug of Bull Durham will soothe Mama every time. "It ain't that kind of a haunting," she offered, just to show her superior knowledge.

I sighed. There isn't much you can do with Mama. Her temper was cooling, though. She ambled around the table and sat down. She can strike a kitchen match with one flick of her thumbnail. She did so now, lighting up a coal oil lamp. We're not wired for electricity because of the expense and because Mama says the fad for it won't last.

"Draw up your chair, and I'll give you a readin'," she says in quite a civil manner, like I'm a customer. There is no charting Mama's moods.

She swept up her pack of cards. There's nobody like Mama for handling a deck. She can shuffle in the air and cut them one-handed. "Take a card, any card," she said, fanning them out on the table.

I turned over the two of clubs, having no doubt she'd give the same reading to any card I happened to draw. There's a lot of show business in Mama.

"Hmmmmm." She squinted at it, then up at me. "That's real interesting, that is," she said, gargling tobacco juice.

"Well, Mama, let's have it. Am I going to make a long journey and meet a handsome stranger?"

Mama doesn't take any sass. "If it's yore fortune

you want to hear, I can give it to you in a nutshell: You won't set down for a week if I catch you near the Old Leverette place. But I ain't doin' a reading on you. That there two of clubs is sending a message. If you don't clam up, I ain't tellin' you what it is."

Between Daisy-Rae and Mama it's a wonder I have any grammar left. Her head began to bob and weave. Her eyes rolled back in her head, which is not a pretty sight.

"Oh, yeah," she muttered, "I hear it clear. Here comes the message from the Great Beyond. Lay it on me!"

I waited patiently, having no choice. At last in a far-off voice she spoke: "*Not all the Unliving are dead!*"

Then she jerked awake. "Where am I? What time is it? What'd I say?"

I sighed. "You said, 'Not all the Unliving are dead!'"

"Did I? Ain't that interesting!"

"If you say so, Mama. Is that the entire message?"

Her eyes squinched to glittering slits. "It's more than enough to them with the Second Sight, which you ain't got much of." She parked her Bull Durham up in her cheek in a final way, so I figured the reading was over.

"Gittin' about suppertime, ain't it?" She glanced over to a bare cupboard and a cold stove. "How does a nice fried chicken sound to you?"

Reaching down on the floor, she fished up a burlap sack and tossed it across the table at me. My heart sank.

"Git a nice plump one," she ordered, "and don't take all night about it."

I took up the sack with a heavy heart. I don't mind doing chores, but I hate rifling around in other people's henhouses every time Mama gets a taste for fried chicken.

"One of these fine nights," I mumbled at the door, "I'll get my head blowed off."

"Keep yore head down," Mama advised. Then, just as I was crossing the threshold, she added, "Who'd you say them two lovebirds was, carryin' on in the woods?"

"That was Miss Mae Spaulding, my old grade—"

"Never mind about her," Mama said. "Who was the dude?"

"Oh, him, he's my history teacher, name of Mr. Ambrose Lacy, and a regular snake in the—"

"I thought I knowed him!" Mama nodded wisely. "He's trouble with a capital *T* and always was!"

Over my shoulder I saw Mama's gaze shoot to her crystal ball to make me think she'd read some special knowledge there. I doubted that, but how she knew of Mr. Lacy I couldn't tell. Mama is not exactly a member of the PTA.

There was no time to ponder this point. "You stick to yore own business," Mama said, sending a jet of brown tobacco juice onto the floor. "Curiosity killed the cat."

But satisfaction brought that cat back, I remarked

to myself as I followed Mama's long, crooked finger pointing out into the night.

An open-sided streetcar, all lit up, clattered past on the tracks outside our house. I followed along in its wake, walking a rail with my sack over my shoulder.

There on the far side of the Armsworth barn, I supposed, Alexander and all the Armsworths were tucking into a good roast beef and mashed potato dinner. Some people have all the luck.

Hoping to make quick work of my chore, I planned to pay a call on the first henhouse I came to. When you're borrowing chickens, it's best to work the other end of town. But I was half-starved, and Mama's temper is short.

As luck would have it, I came up on the back lot of Old Man Leverette's town property. There, beyond a row of dry hollyhocks, was the Leverette privy, and there, at an angle across his punkin patch, the Leverette henhouse.

A light glowed from the window in the kitchen door, but it seemed locked up for the night. I waited a moment in the privy's shadow and then drifted with care across the punkin patch.

Working along a woven-wire fence, I found the gate into the chicken yard and made my way across hen grit and worse. Then I eased open the crude latch on the henhouse door. From within came the little sighs and flutterings of chickens gone to roost.

Nothing you can name smells worse than the inside of a henhouse on a windless night. I slipped inside and waited for my eyes to adjust to the gloom. The Rhode Island Reds were all but invisible on their perches, but the white breeds glowed dimly.

I took a careful step on the slick floor, and a large hen stirred by my ear. The bead of her eye observed me, and I froze. She tucked her head under a wing again. My watchful eye scanned down the row to find one of her sisters less alert.

Chickens aren't the brightest of birds, but easily flustered.

I found a likely specimen, well feathered out. Her beak was tucked beneath her wing, and her neck curved plumply. My hand moved out, fingers itching. In a sudden gesture I had her by the throat, shutting off her wind.

Then things went seriously wrong.

From behind me the henhouse door was nearly wrenched from its hinges. Night air gusted in, and every hen in the place rose up and screamed bloody murder. I turned my particular fowl loose, and she flapped, squawking, away to the rafters.

There's nothing louder than surprised chickens, and the air was white with feathers. I have no doubt they all laid eggs at once. I could have laid one myself.

"REACH FOR THE SKY," a voice roared. "I GOT YOU COVERED." I dropped my sack. It was one of those days.

"TURN AROUND SLOW AND EASY."

As I turned, I saw a great bear-shaped shadow filling the henhouse door. I was also staring into both barrels of a shotgun. "Hold your fire." I sighed. "I am unarmed."

The barrels twitched. "ARE YOU A BOY OR A DWARF?"

"Neither," I answered, somewhat discouraged.

As there's no back way out of a henhouse, I was soon in the open air, which cleared my head, though both barrels were still trained on me.

"Why, there you are, Old—Mr. Leverette," I said quite politely. "I been looking all over the place for you."

"I'LL BET," Old Man Leverette thundered. A rising moon played on his thatch of white hair and whiskers. He's an immense old person, but spry. He squinted at me down his gun barrels. "Durned if you aren't a girl!"

"That's right," I replied, "come to pay you a neighborly call. If you recollect, I dropped in on you last Halloween."

"How many chickens did it cost me that time?" he asked in a threatening voice.

"It was a visit in your best interests. So is this one. Last year I saved your privy from being knocked over. This is your lucky day, as I'm back to do you another good turn."

"If you ain't cool as a cucumber!" Old Man Leverette marveled. His barrels lowered. "Seems like I do recollect a young gal hanging around my privy. What did you say your name was?"

"Letty Shambaugh," I answered, since I always give Letty's name whenever I'm in a tight corner.

He rested his shotgun in the crook of his arm. "Well, Letty, I was just setting to my supper, so talk fast and make it good."

I meant to do my best. "It's like this. Purely by chance I happened to overhear three boys from the high school laying plans to make a regular mess of your front porch and do you an injury the night before Halloween."

"Do tell," Old Man Leverette said. "Who'd you say these boys is?"

"I didn't. Kindly don't interrupt. They mean to set a paper sack of fresh horse manure on the porch floor in front of your door. They're going to ring your bell and set the sack of horse manure afire. Then they'll hide in your shrubbery and watch you run out and stomp on that sack to put the fire out. It could burn your feet and set your nightshirt afire. You could also slip in that mess and break your hip. At your age a broken hip is no joke. Of course, that won't happen now that you've been warned by a responsible person such as myself." I paused to catch my breath.

Old Man Leverette uttered an oath and tugged on his chin whiskers. "The old horse manure stunt," he said in a remembering voice. "We used to pull that one when I was a kid."

"Boys will be boys," I observed, "unless somebody stops them."

"Oh, we'll fix their hash, Letty." A devilish grin lit

up his craggy face. "I suppose you are free the night before Halloween to give me a hand?"

"I can make myself available," I replied, always willing to help out.

"Good." Old Man Leverette then outlined a plan that he devised right there on the spot. It seemed a sure cure for Halloween mischief, and I could see nothing wrong with it.

At that we shook hands on this still-secret plan. I was ready to slip away, but my hand remained locked in Old Man Leverette's big grasp. "If you'll kindly turn me loose," I said, "I'll be on my way."

"You and me has some unfinished business," he rumbled. I felt a sudden chill in the night air. "Chickens."

"Chickens?" I squawked.

Old Man Leverette dragged me out of the henhouse yard and up to his back door. I set my heels, but he was two hundred pounds over my weight.

"Let's us discuss this in a neighborly fashion," I piped. But we'd crossed the threshold into an old-fashioned kitchen. The table was set for one, and the large frying pan on the stovetop was red-hot.

He dragged me to a drainboard. There sat a plump fryer, cut up and rolled in cracker crumbs and ready for the pan. It was even salted and peppered. With his free hand Old Man Leverette reached into a Hoosier cabinet and drew out a checkered napkin.

Then he freed me, saying, "One good turn deserves another. Leave me a drumstick and a thigh, and you can take the rest home in that napkin."

With a pounding heart, I scooped up chicken parts, making short work of this. I was just sailing through the back door when Old Man Leverette raised his voice.

"I bid you good night, Letty, and the next time I catch you anywheres near my henhouse, YOU'LL BE PICKING ROCK SALT OUT OF YOUR BACK END TILL THE DAY OF JUDGMENT."

I cut and ran.

*

At home I found Mama dozing in her chair. Before her, the cards were laid out in a pattern on the table. She'd been telling herself her own fortune, which puts her to sleep every time. She jerked awake in her usual sudden way.

"You took yore sweet time," she snarled. "A person could have died of starvation and bin cool enough to bury."

Her sharp eye fell on the checkered-napkin parcel swinging in my hand. "What in tarnation do you call that?"

"Supper," I replied briefly.

"That ain't no chicken! Let me remind you a chicken's got claws and feathers and a comb and two little beady eyes. Girl, sometimes I wonder if you got good sense."

I unfolded the napkin on the table with a small flourish.

Mama's eyes widened, and her jaw dropped.

"Well, I'll be a . . . It's cut up and ready for the pan. It's even salted and peppered! Girl, how'd you work that?"

"Powers, Mama." I smiled sweetly. "I got wonderful Powers."

7

On my way to school the following day I had much on my mind, as I often do.

There was that son of a gun Mr. Lacy, horsing around with two respectable women of the community. Somebody ought to fix his hash.

There was Alexander Armsworth, who was liable to be shocked senseless by Old Man Leverette's plan to foil the vandalism of his front porch. Unless Alexander was given a timely warning.

There was Mama, as there always is. Her sly hints that something was seriously amiss with the old abandoned Leverette farmhouse nagged at me. If I didn't get to the bottom of that for myself, I'd begin to question my Second Sight.

There was even the freshman fund raiser for the Halloween Festival to plague me. I seemed to have no part in planning it whatsoever. A person doesn't like being left out, especially me.

I decided to tackle Alexander first. As Daisy-Rae says, he's standoffish and getting worse. But I figured I owed him a debt. If I hadn't informed Old

Man Leverette about what him and Bub and Champ were planning, then Alexander wouldn't be about to get the daylights scared out of him.

Besides, after I'd saved him from making a jackass of himself, he'd be the one to owe me a debt. I liked the sound of that.

But when we all filed into homeroom that morning, his desk stood empty. Old baldy-headed Miss Blankenship was just closing her door to latecomers when Alexander slipped in.

He darted up the aisle with his head scrunched down between his shoulders and his eyes on the floor. You talk about sheepish. When he slipped into the seat ahead of me, his ears looked on fire.

He'd have looked different to me anyhow since he had his clothes on. But with so much on my mind, I couldn't think why he was looking hangdog and embarrassed to death.

While roll was being taken, I poked him once between the shoulder blades. "Say there, Alexander," I whispered into his red ear, "I got some real important information for you regarding Old Man—"

"Lemme alone, Blossom," he hissed hatefully out of the side of his mouth. "You and me are not on speaking terms, and that's permanent. Keep out of my way, or I won't be responsible for the consequences. I could wring your scrawny neck, and you know why!"

I blinked at these cruel words. From the corner of

my eye I noticed Letty Shambaugh smiling snidely from her seat.

This is no way to start a day. I drooped through till afternoon, lonely as a cloud. Without Daisy-Rae to call on, I'd have considered quitting school. During history class I drifted down to the girls' rest room.

"It's me, Daisy-Rae," I said in that echoing place.

The door of her stall edged open. While I propped myself up at the sinks, she eased out of her hiding place when she was sure the coast was clear.

"If you don't look like somethun the cat drug in," she remarked. "Why such a long face?"

Daisy-Rae's face is at least as long on her best day, but I let that pass. "If you'd heard how Alexander Armsworth lit into me this morning, you'd know," I told her.

"Well, what can you expect?" Daisy-Rae said. "After he seen you was spyin' on him buck-naked."

"He seen—saw me?"

Daisy-Rae folded her bony arms across her front and nodded. "Wasn't me and Roderick still hidin' up that tree? Yore Alexander caught sight of you scattin' away through the timber. He had no more sense than to tell that Champ and Bub.

"They both blamed Alexander for the whole thing, sayin' you're sweet on him and foller him wherever he goes."

"That's a dad-burned lie," I said.

"I'm only tellin' you what they said," Daisy-Rae replied. "Say, listen, you wouldn't have nothin' on you to eat, would you? I brought me an apple for lunch, but it didn't stick with me."

As it happened, I'd brought a chicken leg, but I'd been too low in my mind to eat it at lunch. I pulled it out of my pocket and handed it over. Daisy-Rae commenced gnawing on it, lint and all. Soon she was chicken fat from ear to ear.

Watching her work over that drumstick reminded me of Old Man Leverette, so I told her all about his plan and my part in it. "Alexander will have to take his chances," I said with some satisfaction, "now that he won't let me warn him."

Daisy-Rae is a good listener, particularly if you feed her. To the sound of her gnawing, I told her all about how Mr. Lacy was two-timing Miss Fuller with Miss Spaulding. Getting more off my chest, I added, "And I don't have a Chinaman's chance of taking part in the Halloween Festival. Seems like Alexander and Letty have got that all sewed up."

"That ain't all they're up to," Daisy-Rae said, throwing the polished bone reluctantly away. "I eavesdropped on them lollygaggin' in the schoolyard at lunch. Yore Alexander and that Letty's going out tonight to one of them moving picture shows."

I bristled. "Well, if that don't—doesn't take the cake!" I said. "She's set her cap for Alexander, and she's using her position as freshman class president to win him. That snake in the weeds Mr. Lacy could take lessons from Letty!"

And Daisy-Rae agreed, which is what friends are for.

*

That's how me and Daisy-Rae and Roderick happened to attend the moving picture show ourselves that very same Friday night.

If rumor had it that I followed Alexander everywhere he went, then so be it. Besides, I wanted to see for myself how that little simp Letty was playing up to him. Being a boy, Alexander is gullible. Some responsible person might have to save him from Letty's clutches.

Moving pictures are the coming thing, and since Bluff City is a progressive place, we have the Bijou Picture Show, which is downtown on the square.

You'd think two country children such as Daisy-Rae and Roderick would be hard up for novelty. But I had to talk fast to persuade her. She swore she'd get lost in town at night and all the bright lights would strike her blind. You talk about backwoodsy.

In the end I had to meet them in the schoolyard at dusk and lead them downtown. When we got there, though, Daisy-Rae's eyes were big as cartwheels at all the lighted-up shopwindows. When we came to Shambaugh's Select Dry Goods Company, she threw on her brakes.

"Would you look at that?" she said, giving me a nudge. "Ladies' housedresses at ninety-eight cents! Prices is going through the roof. And looky here, a buck and a quarter for shoes." She hitched up her patched skirt and examined her boot, which was tied to her foot with baling wire. "Lucky for me I still got plenty wear left in this pair."

Roderick pressed his nose against the shopwindow and took everything in, though I doubt he can read prices.

When we got to the square, we hung around in the shadow of the courthouse across from the Bijou. Soon Alexander arrived with Letty on his arm. He paid her way, and into the show they went. Us three followed unnoticed.

In former times I've snuck into the Bijou free at the stage door. But I had three nickels laid back for a rainy day, which this was. So I treated Daisy-Rae and Roderick. Up over the Bijou entrance was a name written in electric lights:

MISS PEARL WHITE

Daisy-Rae nudged me. "Who might she be?"

"Miss Pearl White? Shoot, Daisy-Rae, she's the most famous moving picture star in North America."

"Well, I ain't never been in one of these places before." Dragging Roderick along, she followed me inside.

The lights were dimming for the organ recital. We lingered at the back till we saw Letty and Alexander in two on the aisle up near the screen. Luck was with us, as the row behind them was empty.

"Easy does it," I muttered to Daisy-Rae. Like two Indian scouts—three, if you count Roderick—we skulked down the aisle and settled silently into seats behind them.

Letty was twitching her little shoulders in a taffeta blouse. Alexander's arm was snaking around her.

"Oh, Alexander, you better not," simpers Letty, "at least till the lights go off."

Daisy-Rae pretended to run her finger down her throat at this sickening scene.

I strained to hear their conversation but only caught snatches. The organ music was swelling up, playing variations on the popular "When You Wore a Tulip and I Wore a Big Red Rose." Still, I heard the odd word or two.

". . . If I do say so myself," Letty remarked, "it is a first-rate idea that nobody but myself would have thought of."

Alexander, who'll agree to anything, nodded. "A Haunted House will show the whole high school there are no flies on the freshman class."

"We can charge a dime admission fee as a fund raiser," smug Letty said. "It will be the best event in the Halloween Festival."

The organ music swelled up to several crescendos, so I was fighting to hear every word there for a while.

". . . A dungeon, naturally," said Letty, ". . . with rubber hose for snakes. A skeleton for one of the closets would be a nice touch. . . ." Et cetera.

Then while I could hear nothing but organ music, they began to elbow one another.

". . . Absolutely not," Letty whined. "You will

have to talk her into it, Alexander. She positively turns my stomach."

"Count me out," said Alexander firmly. "I've dropped Blossom like a bad habit. I'm not speaking to her again. Ever."

But Letty worked her little shoulder nearer Alexander. She reached up and tickled his ear, which went its reddest. "You must make the sacrifice," she said, "in the name of freshman class unity. It's your duty, Alexander, though heaven knows I realize how repulsive and pushy Blossom is."

Next to me Daisy-Rae was making a nasty gesture at Letty's back with one of her fingers. Even Roderick's drooling mouth seemed especially turned down in disgust.

I was spared more of this insulting conversation as the lights went out and the picture began.

At first a public notice was flashed up on the screen:

IF YOU EXPECT TO RATE AS A GENTLEMAN
YOU WILL NOT EXPECTORATE
ON THE FLOOR

Behind us a camera began to grind. Onto the screen flickered the next message:

MISS PEARL WHITE
in the ninth episode of
THE PERILS OF PAULINE

Daisy-Rae nudged me hard. "Which is her name, Pearl or Pauline?"

"Just hush up a minute," I whispered, "and you'll get the hang of it."

"Quiet behind, please," spoke Alexander from the seat ahead.

The whole civilized world knows that in each episode of *The Perils of Pauline*, Pearl White as Pauline defies death and lives to tell the tale. They even flash words on the screen to explain the story, though that's of little use to Roderick.

In Episode Nine, Pauline is fleeing from cannibals down a beach. They're gaining on her, and poor Pauline is about winded. She looks back a lot and runs to beat the band.

Daisy-Rae's fingers closed tight on my arm. Roderick was on the edge of his seat.

The words

PAULINE FLEES INTO THE SURF

flashed on the screen.

She's knee-deep in ocean waves, and the cannibals' spears are flying all around her. Daisy-Rae flinched, and Roderick bobbed and weaved. "She's a goner for sure," Daisy-Rae whispered. But Alexander up ahead didn't shush her this time. Now his arm was creeping around Letty's little shoulders.

Up on the screen Pauline is searching the sea, looking for help.

HELP IS ON THE WAY

Sure enough, out of the sky swoops a hydroplane, a double-winged job skimming the waves.

"Where'd that thing come from?" breathes Daisy-Rae.

Pauline plunges into deep water and begins swimming like a fish. Roderick seemed to be swimming in his seat, throwing his arms around.

A SAFE HAVEN, OR IS IT?

Though the cannibal spears are still whizzing around her, Pauline makes it to the hydroplane and pulls herself up on the wing.

As she staggers into the rear seat, the pilot raises his goggles and grins evilly back at her. He has a slick little mustache and mean eyes.

"I wouldn't trust that dude for a minute," Daisy-Rae remarks, "but I reckon Pauline don't have much choice."

The hydroplane soars into the air, leaving the cannibals behind. Roderick swoops in his seat, turning his arms into hydroplane wings. Alexander begins to nuzzle Letty's neck.

Of course, the hydroplane pilot is Pauline's worst enemy, a two-timer who has deceived her in love.

Since she has already resisted his advances in Episode Eight . . .

HE TAKES HIS REVENGE

The two-timing pilot lights up a cigarette and flicks away the match, which lands on one of the wings.

"Watch out," Daisy-Rae warns. Roderick is all eyes.

The wing smolders and bursts into flames. Pauline sees and clutches her throat. So does Daisy-Rae. The hydroplane begins to wobble. Roderick falls out of his seat but climbs right back into it.

The cowardly pilot stands up, and lo and behold, he's wearing a parachute. In a single bound he jumps from the blazing plane, leaving Pauline defenseless.

CAN PAULINE ESCAPE HER FATE?

"I don't see how!" roars out Daisy-Rae, answering the screen. Roderick is up on the arm of his chair now, riding it like a horse and drooling overtime.

"What a noisy bunch of rough types behind us," Letty remarks to Alexander. "Somebody ought to call the usher and have them thrown out."

The hydroplane goes into a dive. Pauline is trapped in the back seat without a parachute. For some reason, she's now wearing a chiffon scarf, which is blowing far out behind her.

The organ swells up with the sound of a screaming hydroplane, more or less. The ocean looms near as Pauline and her plane go into a spin.

It's too much for Daisy-Rae. There's no point in trying to tell her it's only a show and not real. She comes up out of her seat, shrieking, "THERE AIN'T A MINUTE TO LOSE. SOMEBODY DO SOMETHUN TO HELP THAT PORE GIRL."

Daisy-Rae's flailing elbows accidentally clip the back of Letty's little curly head a nasty whack.

Knocked half out of her seat, Letty says, "This is too much. Alert the usher, Alexander."

He begins to look back—my way. Things are happening so fast now I can hardly think. Besides, Daisy-Rae is hysterical beside me, which is distracting.

As it happens, Roderick, who's brighter than he looks, goes into action.

Just before Alexander turns and sees me behind him, Roderick reaches down into the bib of his little overalls. He draws up one of his mice. A nice plump one with a long gray tail and white whiskers.

Quick as a wink, he reaches forward and drops the rodent down the back of Letty's blouse.

"Oh, Alexander!" she says, striking out at him coyly. "Stop that this minute!"

Alexander throws up both his hands innocently. Then he notices the lump in Letty's blouse. Trapped under that taffeta, the mouse is trying to make its way over Letty's shoulder to freedom. Alexander's eyes grow wide at this moving lump climbing around under Letty's cap sleeve.

Continuing its trip, the mouse seems to lose its footing and falls forward, tumbling into Letty's small bosom.

She looks down, but all I see are the little quivering curls on the back of her head. Then she looks up at Alexander's two free hands. Then the mouse must have started clawing around down in her front.

Letty's plump little fists reach for the sky and grab air. She goes off like a Roman candle.

"SOMEBODY SAVE ME," she whoops. "I AM IN-FESTED." She flies straight out of her chair, clears the row ahead of her, and lands in a heap by the movie screen.

There she does a kind of native dance on her back. Both her hands are jammed down her neckline, and the buttons on her blouse are popping like corn. The audience comes to its feet for a better view, and several applaud.

The organ swells up with variations on "Oh! You Beautiful Doll," and on the screen it says:

RETURN TO THIS THEATER NEXT WEEK
For the THRILLING CONCLUSION

"Let's git while we can." I elbow Daisy-Rae into action. Us three scramble out of our seats and up the aisle.

But I chance a backward glance, and my heart sinks. There's Alexander standing in his row with his hands on his hips in a disgusted pose, looking daggers right at me.

8

NEXT WEEK AT THE HIGH SCHOOL, word of the upcoming Halloween Festival was on every tongue. The halls were decorated with orange and black streamers and twisted crepe paper. All in all, the mood of the place was more festive than my own.

You could learn of each fund raiser class project by reading the various bulletin boards down the main hall, which I did. The seniors were giving a costume ball with a live band at the hotel downtown. The juniors, trying to copy the seniors, were also giving a dance, but in the gym. The sophomores were planning a wienie roast and hayride.

I came at last to a ladder with Tess and Bess, the Beasley twins, on it. They were tacking up the freshman fund raiser poster. I supposed this was their job as sergeants at arms.

The poster, decorated with several jack-o'-lanterns and black cats, read:

FRESHMAN CLASS HAUNTED HOUSE
Enter If You Dare

and

Have the Living Daylights Scared Out of You

❖

Experience: the dank dungeon and the
bat-filled attic

❖

Hear: clanking chains and unexplained sobs

❖

See and Touch: the ghastly remains of former
victims

❖

Also: spiders, snakes, and other attractions
Many Will Enter, but Few Will Survive
Admission 10¢ as a charitable contribution

signed, Letty Shambaugh,
Freshman Class President

While I was reading this corn-fed poster, Tess and
Bess with tack hammers in their hands looked down
from their ladder.

"Why, good morning, Blossom honey," they said
in chorus. They often try to speak together like a
tuneless duet. I looked up in surprise, as I'm not
used to being spoken to by members of Letty's club.

"Isn't a Haunted House the cleverest idea you
ever heard of?" said Tess or Bess.

"We'll be scared to death, literally," the other one
said.

That would be no great loss, I thought. Wandering on, I smelled a rat, as I often do.

As I entered homeroom, Miss Blankenship was

lettering her daily message from *Hamlet* on the board:

TO BE OR NOT TO BE:
THAT IS THE QUESTION
Act III

Halloween or not, Miss Blankenship is always business as usual. Letty was absent. It was Wednesday, and she'd been absent all week, no doubt suffering the lingering effects of mouse infestation.

But Alexander soon entered. He strode down the aisle with shoulders squared. His ears were hardly pink, and his hair was slicked down with Vitalis hair preparation. As I have mentioned, he is not a bad-looking kid.

"Good morning, Blossom." He nodded civilly.

I flinched. Alexander slipped into his desk chair, arranging his pens and setting out his schoolbooks in neat order.

Something is rotten, I thought, *in the state of—*

"Say, listen, Blossom." His head swiveled to me. "What is your opinion of our Haunted House class project?"

"It will prove without doubt that there are no flies on the freshmen," I mocked.

He blinked. "That's what I thought, too." He turned away, but not for long. "By the way, Blossom—"

"I thought you and me weren't speaking, Alexander."

"Oh, that," he said. "I'm not one to carry grudges

and hope you are the same. We have the unity of the freshman class to consider."

"Is that a fact."

Alexander nodded, making a full turn. "How would you like to take part in running the Haunted House?"

I shot him a dangerous look. "How would you like to—"

But the first bell sounded then, and Miss Blankenship turned on us.

"Meet me under the shade tree in the schoolyard at lunch," Alexander whispered importantly. "We'll discuss the matter."

Like Hamlet himself, I could hardly make up my mind all morning. As I was not born yesterday, I knew Alexander was playing up to me only under Letty's orders. For reasons of her own, she'd decided I was to be in on the class fund raiser. I decided to play along just to see what they were up to.

At lunch I awaited Alexander under the shade tree. Daisy-Rae's broken boots were dangling down from a branch, so at least I'd have a witness.

Alexander strolled up. "Well, Blossom, here is the deal. Letty—several of us officers have decided on the various attractions for our Haunted House. Tess and Bess, dressed up as bats, will flit around in the attic. Ione and Harriet and several others will jump out of closets at people. And we're going to dress Champ Ferguson up as a monster, and—"

"Champ Ferguson isn't a freshman," I reminded him.

"I know, but he's almost six foot tall, and we need a monster that size. Nobody'll know him when we get him disguised."

"And what part are you playing in this, Alexander?"

He drew himself up. "I'm in charge of the dungeon, which is in the cellar. I'll be leading customers around in the dark down there and letting them feel the deadman's remains. We'll have a couple of peeled grapes for his eyes and a wet sponge for his brain and some warm spaghetti for his guts and—"

"Hold it," I said. "I've heard enough. Where do I come in on this deal?"

"You'll be the star attraction," he said, "sort of."

"Is that a fact."

"Sure. You're to dress up like a witch—you can borrow some of your mama's clothes—and tell people's fortunes. We'll charge them an extra nickel for the reading."

I gave this some thought. Considering the other corn-fed plans they had for their so-called Haunted House, they could use a star attraction. And they knew it, too. It's a sight how agreeable people can be when they want something out of you.

"Of course," Alexander said, "you can just fake the fortune-telling part."

I bristled. "Fake it? What for? I'll remind you, Alexander, I got Powers and the Second Sight, same as you. You know yourself me and you can see the Unseen and glimpse Other Worlds if we put our minds to it."

"Well, just hush up about that," Alexander said, glancing nervously around. "I have left all that kind of thing behind me, and I don't care to discuss it. Besides, I don't think we have those powers anymore." He cleared his throat. "I haven't been troubled in that way for quite a spell now. I expect it was just a stage that we have outgrown."

"Is that a fact," I replied. "Gimme your hand."

He thrust both his hands into his pockets.

"Gimme your hand, and be quick about it." When I got him to stretch out a hand, I turned it palm up and ran my fingers lightly over it, squinting hard.

"Hmmmmm," says I, "that's real interesting, that is."

"Knock it off, Blossom."

"Oh, yes, I see it clear now." I pointed at random to a little line running across his palm. "Danger lurks in your immediate future."

"Cut it out, Blossom."

"No question about it," I said. "I see . . . I see a dark and windswept night. Not Halloween. No. Sooner than that." Alexander's hand quivered in mine. "I see two—no, three shadowy figures. And . . . what's this? A porch! That's it, a porch. I see these three figures carrying something . . . a sack. PEEE-YEW," I said. "It stinks. I see these three figures carrying this smelly sack up onto the porch."

I checked Alexander's face to see how he was taking this. His eyes were growing wary and dark.

"I see these three figures touching a match to this

nasty sack . . . in front of the door. They're laughing like fools and punching each other on the arms. They're ringing the doorbell now and scampering off the porch. But lo and behold! Something they didn't expect is about to—"

Alexander grabbed his hand away. His ears were burning bright, and his friendly mood was forgotten.

"Very funny, Blossom," he sneered. "As if I didn't know where you came by that information."

"It's all there in your hand, Alexander. As you can see, I'm a first-rate fortune-teller. I could tell more if I felt like it, which I don't."

"You're a first-rate snoop, Blossom. You've snooped on me at the . . . swimming hole, and you've snooped on me at the Bijou Picture Show. My life is hardly worth living, you spidery-legged little—"

"Hold it right there, Alexander." I spoke sternly. "If you get on the wrong side of me, where will you be with Letty? Me and you both know she sent you to sweet-talk me into telling fortunes. It has taken you quite a while to get up your nerve, too, and it's Wednesday already. We are but two days from Halloween, and if you fail in your mission, your name will be mud with Letty. Give it some thought!"

He did.

"For two cents," he muttered, "I'd resign as vice-president. It's not worth the grief."

"Never mind," I said. "This is your lucky day, as I'm willing to overlook your foul temper. I reckon I can make myself available as fortune-teller. Where are you setting up this so-called Haunted House anyway?"

Looking relieved, Alexander said, "Oh, it's ready-made, and we're decorating it real good. We're using the old abandoned Leverette farmhouse out in the country."

My eyes no doubt popped. "How's that again, Alexander?"

"The old broken-down farmhouse," he explained, "out past the—ah—swimming hole."

I swallowed. "I see. Well now, that puts a new light on things."

Alexander eyed me. "You can't back out now, Blossom. You gave your word."

"Maybe so, but I also gave my word to Mama that I'd never go near that place."

"I will grant you," Alexander said, "that your mama is crazy as a loon and mean as a weasel, but what has she got against that old falling-down house?"

"Don't you know, Alexander?"

"No," he said, but he was looking shifty.

"Mama says that place is haunted or something. I mean, *really* haunted."

"There you go again, Blossom, telling tall tales and lying through your teeth."

"I didn't say a word about it, Alexander. I don't know what particular problem the old Leverette farmhouse suffers from. But I tell you one thing: It suffers from *something*. Mama doesn't kid around."

"In that case," he said, "why don't you just sneak off on Halloween night and don't tell your mama where you're going? The whole town knows you've done that type thing before."

"I might and I might not," I replied. "But I know one thing, Alexander. I'm going to find out what ails that place. It would be a rich joke indeed if the freshman class tried to run a fake Haunted House in a real one. Before I commit myself to telling any fortunes in that place, I mean to find out the truth."

"You do that." Alexander jittered. "You check it out and let me know your decision." He turned then, ready to cut out.

"Not so fast, Alexander. Me and you are going out to the old Leverette place tonight—after dark. With our particular Powers, we ought to be able to plumb its deepest mysteries."

Alexander was shaking his head briskly. "No, you don't, Blossom. You don't drag me into one of your harebrained schemes. You've made up this whole thing to get me alone somewheres. Count me out, and that's final!"

"Very well, Alexander, and maybe you can get Letty Shambaugh to tell fortunes on Halloween night, as I will not be available."

And that's how me and Alexander Armsworth happened to pay a visit in the dead of that very night out to the old Leverette farmhouse beyond Leverette's Woods, to learn for ourselves if that strange place concealed some eerie mystery beneath its sagging roof.

9

It was a dark and windswept night, and Alexander was in one of his sulks. He slouched along the country road with a railroad lantern in the crook of his arm and took long strides, trying to outdistance me. Our shadows were long on the road in the light of the bobbing lantern. His only conversation was grunts.

By and by we came along past Leverette's Woods, where the wind was thrashing the treetops. "The entrance to Lovers' Lane is right around here somewheres," I pointed out.

"Oh, no, you don't," Alexander said. "You won't get me into any Lovers' Lane. We'll go around by the pasture." So we were soon waist-high in unmown grass, proceeding across the pasture Indianfile. I had a job to keep up. Alexander wouldn't have minded giving me the slip.

He slowed when the sloping roof of the old Leverette place loomed ahead of us. Then he dropped down in the weeds so quick I nearly fell over him.

"I tripped over a stone," he said, though I didn't see one.

"We better keep moving," I said. "It's cold, and besides, you're going to set the grass afire with that lantern if you're not careful."

"Nag, nag, nag," said Alexander. "I twisted my ankle."

Across the moon an owl flew with some small creature in its claws. The lightning rods on the roof of the old house pointed like daggers at the black sky. From beyond the place came the sighing of a wind pump turning in the breeze. I smelled rain in the air and sensed a storm.

I heard something else then, I swear I did. Clear on the night air, it was a peculiar *pyong, pyong, pyong* with the occasional *beep*. Coming and going, it sent some strange signal.

But I couldn't place it. It was nothing I knew or quite earthly. From the corner of my eye I checked Alexander to see if he'd heard it, too. But it was dark in the weeds, and the lantern seemed to burn lower.

"I think my ankle's swelling. My sock feels tight."

"You'd better give that ankle some exercise," I said, starting up. But as I took my next step toward the house, I froze in my tracks.

All of the many windows in the old abandoned Leverette place were like dead eyes. Except for a window upstairs beneath the drooping drainpipe. From a single room came a dim blue light, flickering, pulsing.

Pyong, I heard distantly. *Pyong, pyong, beep.* A sudden wind went through me, or something did. The racing clouds cleared the moon, and I saw something on the roof among the lightning rods. It was some strange arrangement of rods and sticks stuck up on a small pole. But it faded while I watched.

Then, just for an instant, the whole place glowed. From every window in the house white light poured, throwing pale shapes on the untended yard.

It was electric light, but of course, the old Leverette place had never been wired for electricity. Old Man Leverette doesn't even have electricity in his residence in Bluff City. I blinked, and the house went black again. Maybe a little blue sparked from the upstairs window again, then utter darkness.

I settled back in the weeds beside Alexander. He was bent low, examining his ankle. Or hiding his eyes. I decided to wait until he'd gathered what courage he had.

The old wind pump sighed again. Dry leaves scudded out in swirls from the woods. Just to liven up Alexander a little, I spoke the following lines in a spooky voice, right in his ear:

" 'Tis now the very witching time of night,
When churchyards yawn and hell itself breathes out
Contagion to this world. . . ."

All of Alexander's hair seemed to stand up on his head. Even his beanie quivered. "Would you shut up with that kind of talk. Where'd you get it anyhow?"

"It's *Hamlet*," I explained, "Act Three. Don't you ever read the blackboard?"

"This isn't English class," he snapped, "so cut it out. It's getting late, and I'd better be getting—"

"You're right," I said fast. "We'd better conduct our investigation. We wouldn't want midnight to find us in *that* place."

I jumped up and headed for the house, as brave as possible under the circumstances. Alexander had no choice but to follow. Thunder rolled out of the distance, following a lightning flash.

At the top of a flight of wooden steps the porch was in deep shadow. Dead autumn leaves crunched beneath our boots, and Alexander tried to take charge. He held the lantern aloft at the front door. Over it a sign had recently been tacked up. It was orange cardboard with squiggly black letters that read:

REPENT WHAT'S PAST;
AVOID WHAT IS TO COME

"Tess and Bess did that sign for the entrance," Alexander explained. "It's a nice, scary motto."

"It's from *Hamlet*," I said, "also Act Three." We stepped inside, Alexander politely letting me go first.

In the front hall the lantern threw red light across curling wallpaper and up a long stairway. "Here's where we'll collect the admission fees," Alexander said in a breaking voice. "We'll have a couple jack-o'-lanterns around for light. The cobwebs are real."

I touched his sleeve to quiet him. We stood in that

shadowy place while I listened to the house. If I started Vibrating and picking up messages with my inner ear and my special Powers, I wanted to be close to the front door. But I heard nothing except the wind in the eaves and a spatter of rain in the gutters. Far off, a loose shutter clapped against the house.

"Quit listening," Alexander muttered. "You're just asking for trouble."

Never a step ahead of me, he gave us a tour. The dining room was bare except for trash and an old-fashioned gasolier fixture hanging down from the ceiling.

"Harriet Hochhuth is going to hang in that china closet over there. We're going to string her up with wires as an artificial corpse."

Alexander scooted through a door, taking the lantern and leaving me in darkness. "This here's the kitchen," he hollered. I skipped on into the so-called kitchen, which was a filthy mess.

"We're going to stretch Champ Ferguson out on this drainboard," Alexander explained, "and disguise him as a monster, which we're sewing together from spare parts found in a graveyard. There'll be a big bucket of grape juice for blood. That's one of my own crackerjack ideas.

"And over there"—Alexander pointed—"are the stairs to the cellar, where we're setting up the dead-man's dungeon and model torture chamber." He turned his back on the black cellar stairs, making it clear he wasn't going down there tonight.

"Where am I to tell my fortunes?" I asked. "I wouldn't mind a well-aired spot. This kitchen smells like a bear's breath."

"You'll be upstairs in one of the bedrooms," Alexander said in an offhand way. "We don't have time to wander around up there."

He was more than ready to leave right then.

"Listen, Alexander," I said, "we've come out here to give this house a thorough investigation. We aren't going to learn a thing with a quick look around a couple of rooms."

He sulked.

"It's all right if you're afraid to go upstairs with me," I said. "I understand."

I had him there. He wasn't about to hang around down here all by his lonesome. His imagination was already working overtime.

We were in the dining room again as Alexander edged toward the front door. He knew he was going to have to go upstairs with me, but he was putting it off. Setting the lantern on the floor, he reached down to rub his so-called twisted ankle.

Suddenly, right behind him, I saw a small wink of light, bright in the lantern glow. I'd like to have turned to stone. My mouth fell open. Alexander happened to notice my bugging eyes.

Slowly, slowly he turned to look behind himself, his face as white as this page. The brass knob on the china closet door was winking in the light and turning.

My boots seemed nailed to the floor, and Alexander began to sway. Still the knob kept turning, all by itself.

Squeaking on its hinges, the door opened upon the blackness of a tomb within. Peering from inside was a frightful sight, a face not quite human in the flickering lantern flame. It appeared to be an ungrinning skull.

"Oh, I will be a good boy for the rest of my life," Alexander moaned, "if only this isn't happening!"

He sagged, but he couldn't run any more than I could. The ghastly little face looked up into Alexander's tear-filled eyes. The terrible little mouth drooled. It was Roderick.

He stepped out of the china closet in his small pair of bib overalls.

"What say, Roderick?" I greeted him, though my mouth was dry. Roderick looked us over but said nothing.

"Who," moaned Alexander, "who in the—"

But the kitchen door banged open then, sending a shudder through the house. Footsteps stalked, and another fearful apparition appeared in the dining room door. Alexander's head swiveled toward this new horror. He grabbed his throat.

Daisy-Rae marched in. "There you are, you little rascal!" She was wearing a feed sack nightgown and a nightcap of faded flannelette. Sweeping Alexander aside, she made a grab for Roderick and hooked him by the ear.

"Ain't I told you time and agin not to slip off? It's a-way past your bedtime!"

Alexander's eyes were like saucers, and in truth, Daisy-Rae in her night togs is a sight. He managed to stand clear of her flailing elbows as she nearly shook Roderick loose from his ear.

"Who," Alexander moaned again, "who in the—"

"Hey there, Blossom," Daisy-Rae said, nodding her wan face at me.

"Hey there, Daisy-Rae," I replied.

"Be glad you ain't got any little brothers," she said. "They are a continual worry. It's my own fault. I had no more sense than to tell Roderick here that you and yore Alexander was coming over tonight to check over this place for haunts. Naturally the little scamp had to spy on you. You know how he is." Roderick's neck seemed permanently bent, but she never turned him loose.

Out of the room she marched, quick as she'd come. Roderick scampered by her side, trying to keep up with his ear. The back door banged behind them as off they went to their chicken coop home.

After a long pause Alexander spoke. "Don't tell me. I don't even want to know."

*

Delay it though he would, it was time to explore upstairs. The thought of those throbbing blue lights in the upper window skated past my mind. But I planted a firm foot on the stairs, keeping Alexander by me. Thunder crashed above the attic. Lantern light wobbled on the treads as we climbed up through the house. The things that live in walls skittered, seeming to warn one another. Cobwebs swept our beanies and caressed our ears.

Where the stairs curved at the top, I dropped back a little just to see how far ahead of me Alexander would go. The ceiling had fallen up there, so he crunched along a step or two over broken plaster, holding his lantern high.

Alexander opened the first door he came to and banged it shut again. Making a strangled sound, he took flight and shot into the next room he saw. After a moment he spoke in a hollow voice. "Now here is a good room for your fortune-telling, Blossom. Yes, this will do very well."

I was standing in the upstairs hall. Even without the lantern I could still see. My gaze fell to the door Alexander had opened and closed so quick. There was a line of light under it, bright across the dusty hall floor.

It glowed like daylight but whiter. To save my soul I couldn't walk past that door. I looked back down the curving stairs into blackness.

"Get in here, Blossom!" Alexander called out from a far room. "Don't go near that door! You hear me? There's something there. I don't know what, but . . . something."

I hardly heard him. Everything faded except for the light beneath the mystery door. All by itself my hand reached for the knob.

10

LIGHTNING SPLIT THE AIR, traveling down the rods on the roof. It clamped my hand to the doorknob. I couldn't turn loose or turn back now. My skin sizzled, and the door blew in, jerking me half out of my boots.

Inside, the light like a white fog peeled my eyeballs and took me prisoner. The sounds I'd heard in the distance were clearer and nearer: the *pyongs* and the *beeps* alike. They were no noise of nature or the human voice.

Suddenly I was free of the electrified doorknob, so I threw up my hands, thinking I'd be burned by the light. But it was cold. Then I was drawn like an autumn leaf into a funnel of brightness. I swam in this spiral, never trying to breathe. My kinky hair flattened against my skull as I gathered speed. My spelling medal flapped like a loose shutter against my chest.

I seemed to shriek, though no one heard, not even me. But my thoughts cried out. *Oh, Mama, you were right. I never should have come near this place....*

But it was too late. Whatever was to befall me now was happening already.

I traveled in a great void past thunder and beyond lightning. But I wasn't alone, far from it. Looming up from every side were creatures far worse than any in Alexander's dungeon or model torture chamber. There were circular monsters that were all mouth. There were creatures with lights for eyes and steel for skin who wielded long glowing tubes of light for swords. Their dreadful jaws snapped at me in passing, and those bright swords of light tried to snag me. But I hurtled on.

Then, don't ask me how, I was swimming up through dry waters. Square ahead of me stretched a glassy skin like the ice on a pond as seen by a fish. I rocketed nearer this cruel barrier, expecting to batter out my brains.

In an explosion of ice or glass, I burst through. Gasping with my first breath, I did a neat somersault in real air and fell flat on my back on a carpeted floor. My eyeteeth were all jarred loose. Though I was as dizzy as a swung cat, I tried to raise up on my elbows.

Looking toward a door, I saw I was still in the old Leverette place. The bedroom door was painted now, but I knew the knob. Though I saw where I was, I'd fallen out of my time. Or I'd been pushed.

"Oh, wow," said a voice quite near me. "I've pushed DELETE and RETURN. What more can I do?"

*

My beanie was over my ear, but my mind was clearing. Cautiously I scanned the bright room. A bookshelf without books held long rows of narrow boxes in bright colors.

Beside them was a sight that made me shrink. It was a creature nearly my height. I'd seen it not moments before, or a near cousin to it, hurtling through space. It had a cast-iron face and a long tube of glowing light that it brandished for a sword.

I chanced another look at this specimen. It was only a large, air-filled doll. The wicked iron face was painted onto a slick skin that may have been rubber. It was a monster-shaped toy or perhaps a work of art. There is no accounting for taste.

My shifting glance fell upon a wall calendar. It was decorated with more monsters conducting warfare in tin airships. But it was the date on the calendar that burned my brain.

I raised a trembling hand to count on my fingers. Arithmetic is not my best subject, but from the year on the calendar I saw I'd slipped ahead near enough . . . seventy years.

My eyes dropped to the floor. There was someone in the room with me. I'd known that right along. I was stretched out beside a table and chair. There were several legs, two of them human.

Planted on the carpet were two things of white rubber and colored canvas. Figuring they were shoes, I took a closer look. Written on these so-called shoes were little words:

ADIDAS

I chanced a look up the legs. They weren't long and were covered by ordinary blue denim work pants, somewhat farmerish. Well worn, too. I craned my neck to read a small announcement stitched to the seat:

SEARS TOUGHSKINS

Still, nothing moved but me. Above the pants was a plain cotton shirt stretched over a boy's torso. It was short-sleeved of the undershirt variety. I was up on my knees now beside the occupied chair. This undershirt was lettered boldly across the chest:

PAC-MAN FEVER

I looked up into the face of a boy.

He was a kid of thirteen or so—eighth grade, tops. Except he would not be born for many years. I knew that much. His cheeks were freckled, and a shock of red hair hung on his forehead. Propped on his nose were spectacles that gave him a learned look.

He sat at a desk before the keyboard of a thing like a typewriting machine. There were other buttons and a lever before him and a variety of metal boxes. One of them contained a window with a small curl of gray smoke rising out of the shattered pane. That was where I'd entered this particular world.

The boy looked worried. My nose was near his thigh, since I'd been reading his outfit. Being a boy, he was trying to be brave. Still, his elbow edged away from me, though he seemed rooted to his chair.

"Oh, wow," he said again. "And they call this model state-of-the-art." Somewhat disgusted, he smacked the keyboard of his machine with the heel of his hand. "I guess I could try the CLEAR key or maybe GOTO. They promised open-ended options, but this is ridiculous."

"You can say that again," I remarked.

That moved him. He jerked up his Adidas feet and grabbed himself. "You can *talk*," he gasped.

"And what's more, I can make sense," I replied, "which is more than you're doing."

"Wow," he pondered, "I didn't think even Atari had the chips for speech yet. I hadn't counted on a voice option. I can't seem to get a fix on this model." He gave the keyboard another thump.

"It's an off brand," he went on, "a loaner from off the showroom floor. Its hardware is fairly primitive, and I can't say much for its peripherals. I traded in my Atari 2600 VCS, which is somewhere between obsolescent and obsolete. Now I'm waiting to take delivery on the 5200, which is basically a teen toy and actually reasonably sophisticated for adult games. I'm in the Gifted Program myself."

"Is that a fact," I said. "You speak any English?"

He blinked at me in wonder and rubbed his chin in thought. "I guess I sort of . . . made you happen," he remarked. "In the Career Discovery module at school I'm already locked into Systems Analysis as a life's work, but now I wonder. With you, I guess I sort of looped when I should have branched. Where'd you come from?"

"Bluff City," I answered cautiously.

He nodded. "You do look sort of inner-city. But what I meant was, what *game* are you from?"

One of his fingers edged out to press a key on his board. He seemed to think he had to push certain buttons to make me talk sense.

"I mean, like, are you from Berzerk or Demons to Diamonds or Donkey Kong or Chopper Command or what?"

"Listen, bud," I replied, "this is getting us nowhere."

"Let me put it this way," he said. "We can always erase if we aren't achieving interface. Are you composed of electronic impulses, or are you just a bug in my flow chart?" He slapped his machines again. "I'm going to have to know where to store you. In this model I've only got sixteen K of RAM."

"RAM?" I inquired.

He blinked again. "Random Access Memory."

"Let's look at this whole thing another way," I said. "And hold off on that talk about erasing me. I've been through enough already. Where I came from, we were having an electrical storm. Thunder, lightning—you follow me?"

"We were having a storm, too," he said, "but it's clearing off now." He jerked his head toward a window, but I dared not yet look outdoors into more of his world. "Maybe it was the same storm?" He rubbed his chin in thought once more.

"Maybe," I said, more cautious than before.

Through the round spectacles his eyes searched me. "What's that thing on top of your . . . hair?"

I reached up slowly. A steel helmet with horns and a flashing light wouldn't have surprised me. But it was only my beanie, hanging by a hatpin.

He squinted at me. "You sure you're not a game component? You know, an animation. Your . . . hat has numbers on it. What does eighteen stand for? That doesn't compute with me."

Well, of course, there were numbers on my beanie, same as any other freshman's. "That's our graduation year," I said without thinking. "We graduate from Bluff City High School in 1918." My mouth clamped shut on this information. It seemed to seal my fate.

"Oh, wow," the boy breathed, and thunder rolled over distant hills. The metal box before him emitted a single *pyong* and then a solitary *beep*.

*

There was nothing simple about my situation, but it boiled down to this. My Second Sight and the lightning and maybe something else had ganged up on me. I'd slipped through time into the distant decade of the 1980s without leaving this upstairs room of the old abandoned Leverette farmhouse.

But in this future world the farmhouse was abandoned no longer. Somebody had remodeled the old place, making it strictly modern and then some. This upstairs bedroom was now occupied by a boy named Jeremy. Though he managed to introduce himself, he was still halfway convinced that he'd created me in his machines, "programmed me," as he kept saying. He even made me acquainted with his equipment, his "power supply transformer" and his "television interface box," his "joystick" and his "paddles." You never heard such gibberish.

When I could get a word in, I said, "You can call me Blossom."

"Outrageous," he replied. "You got to be kidding. That's better than Tron." He slapped a knee and chortled.

"Listen, buster—Jeremy, this is no laughing matter. What we have here is a serious problem. I happen to have considerable Powers of the occult type and have wandered out of my time before. But never this far."

Jeremy waved a hand. "Oh, I got that figured. My black box has been malfunctioning all evening. The electrical storm—maybe two storms, one at your end and one at mine—messed up my computer's head. It picked up on you. Due to a long shot circuitry-wise, you basically just slipped into a time warp."

"A what?"

"It's a well-known phenomenon," Jeremy replied. "You're definitely not up on your Ursula Le Guin, your Isaac Asimov, or your Madeleine L'Engle, are you?"

"Not entirely," I muttered, figuring these three probably hadn't been born yet.

"The time warp is in all the sci-fi literature as a distinct potential, so it stands to reason, doesn't it?" He spoke confidently, but his eyes weren't so sure.

I creaked up from the carpet, bruised both fore and aft. Tripping through a time warp is similar to falling out of a tree. My gray princess dress, which I wear for every day now, and an old coat of Mama's with a ratty fur collar were half wrenched off my body.

Jeremy gave my togs an interested stare. "Funky," he remarked. "Is your gear recycled?"

But I'd turned from where he sat to the door with the familiar knob. Hoping against hope, I thought that beyond the door I might find myself again in the plaster-strewn hall of the old abandoned Leverette place. Just maybe Alexander might be out there, holding his lantern aloft in the dark, waiting for me.

Limping across the room, I peered around the door. The hallway was brightly lit. The floor was smooth with polish. High on the opposite wall was a round device with a small red light in it. Written on this object was a motto:

SMOKE ALERT

I glanced down the curving stairs. On the window at the landing was another motto, glued to the glass:

THIS HOUSE PROTECTED
BY ELECTRONIC SURVEILLANCE

I banged the door shut. All escape was cut off.

Not far from panic, I raced back across the room to the dreaded window. Sweeping curtains aside, I stared out into the night. Icy fingers of fear gripped my vitals.

"The wind pump," I whispered, "it's gone. And right about there should be the chicken coop where Daisy-Rae lives with her little brother, Roderick."

"Who?" said Jeremy softly.

"And the woods. They ought to be right over there, with the little gate to Lovers' Lane. Why, me and Mama have all but lived off them woods in lean times, what with the hickory nuts and squirrel stew."

"Squirrel what?" asked Jeremy.

But where all these familiar landmarks should be was a blanket of twinkling lights as far as the eye could see. Just where the gate to the woods should be two paved streets crossed.

Above them was an electrified lantern, sending out a beam of green light. As I watched, it was joined briefly by a yellow light. Then they blew out, and on came a red one. I shivered at this strange signal.

There was a house on every corner, glowing with white light. On each roof was an elaborate lightning rod or something very like one. In the distance beyond the ruined woods where the swimming hole should be were two brightly lighted golden arches and a sign blazing white fire that read:

McDonald's
40 Billion Sold

Clutching my forehead, I turned to the boy.

"Don't tell me Bluff City's grown all the way out here, Jeremy. Why, we're a couple of miles from the Courthouse Square!"

"Bluff City?" he said. "Oh, we never go there. There's not much to Bluff City except parking lots and urban renewal. Where we are is Bluffleigh Heights, basically one of your better upper-middle-class suburbs."

"I see," I said untruthfully. "Then I take it you don't go to Horace Mann School?"

"Where?" said Jeremy. "I'm in eighth grade at Bluffleigh Heights Magnet Middle School. I'm in the Gifted Program."

"So you said," I remarked. "And what does the Gifted Program mean . . . basically?"

"It means we're all reading at or near grade level and pretty heavy into computer math."

I gave this some thought. "You mean you can do your homework on that . . . computer thing?" I jerked a thumb at his machines.

"How else?" Jeremy gave his black box a small pat. "Homework, of course," he said, "and video games."

"Games?"

"I've got them all: Yar's Revenge, The Empire Strikes Back, Kaboom, Star Strike, Night Stalker,

Moon Master, Defender, Atlantis, you name it. Here I've got real arcade action, you know?

"I was up to here with coin-op games. Now I don't even have to leave the house except to go to school. And we're hoping for a breakthrough even there. I foresee the time when we can hook into a master control and attend classes without even getting out of bed. You could completely Betamax your absenteeism, you know?

"I mean the technology's there already. It's just a matter of breaking through an entrenched bureaucracy and knocking out the power of the athletic department that wants you actually there up in the stands, supporting the teams. Basically it's just a question of time before—"

It was no good. I had no doubt Jeremy was making sense in his way, but I was only catching every other word. At least he was a human being and not a monster with a metal face or that big blown-up dummy that stood under his calendar.

I noticed something else in Jeremy, too, for figuring out people is one of my Gifts. He was a lonesome boy up in his room surrounded by his machines and creatures. It was a lonely place, this future.

The thought brought a couple of rare tears to my eyes. I'd never had a favored position even in my own world of 1914. But I missed it now. The homesickness for my vanished place flooded through me and spilled out at my eyes.

"I've got to get back, Jeremy. I'm needed elsewhere. I've got to get back to teach Alexander and Bub and Champ a lesson when they pull that prank on Old Man Leverette's porch tomorrow night. I've got to get back and straighten out that two-timing Mr. Lacy, who's sparking Miss Spaulding and Miss Fuller all at once. I've got to get back and tell fortunes at our freshman class Haunted House. Halloween's the day after tomorrow!"

Jeremy blinked at me through his round spectacles, as I pointed out into the night. I have a long and bony forefinger which I inherited from Mama. I pointed it out into the dreadful, glittering night of Bluffleigh Heights.

"Home . . ." I moaned in a strangled voice.

Jeremy rubbed his chin, deep in thought. His gaze dropped to a small white instrument among the other machines on his desk. It had a curly cord and a small barbell arrangement resting on a stand with small numbered buttons. "I don't suppose you could . . . phone . . ." he mumbled.

Then far down in the house a door banged. Heavy footsteps stamped up the stairs.

Jeremy quivered, and his gaze darted to the door. "Oh, wow," he said.

11

"WITH ANY LUCK," Jeremy said in a low voice, "it'll be Mom, home from her Parents Without Partners meeting."

"And without any luck?" I wondered.

"It'll be my sister." He spoke in a grave voice and wrung his hands. "What am I going to *do* with you?"

He sized me up again, though he'd been staring holes in me ever since I . . . arrived. "Quick," he said, "get over by my Darth Vader."

"Your what?"

"That plastic thing." He pointed at the artificial monster. "Stand over by it, and don't move. Hold your pose. *Freeze*."

Just as the doorknob rattled, I lifted my skirts and took a giant leap, landing next to the Darth doll. It was staring out at the room, and suddenly so was I. Me and it stood cheek to cheek. The door banged back.

Somehow Jeremy made it to his chair. Looking up with a casual air, he said, "Hi, Tiffany. What are you doing home? Did the mall close?"

An overfed girl of sixteen or so shambled into the room. Without shifting my eyeballs, I caught a terrifying glimpse of her.

She'd cut her skirt in two, for it hit her well above two large and naked knees. Over her big chest she wore a flimsy shirt with some small animal stitched to the left side, possibly an alligator.

Her face was made up for some dreadful stage drama, purple at the lips and green along the lids. But her hair was worse. It was plucked half out of her head and chopped off. Wisps at the side were dyed pink. She wore earphones like a telephone company operator.

"HEY, TIFFANY," Jeremy roared, "HOW ABOUT GETTING OUT OF MY ROOM?"

She was a slow girl and possibly deaf. She pulled the plug from one of her ears. Like my mama, she pierced her ears. But . . . Tiffany had pierced hers three times on each side. Gaudy bangles hung down from her lobes.

"Just shut up for like one minute, you little space cadet," she remarked to Jeremy. "I'm totally into Billy Joel's 'The Nylon Curtain.'" She was tapping one large foot in a rhythm, and so she may have been getting music from out of her earplugs, or thought she was. "'Combat Rock' with Clash is coming up."

"Just . . . get . . . outta . . . my . . . room, okay?" Jeremy said to her. "Please."

"Chill out, nerd," she responded. "Have a Dorito."

She slouched across the room and offered a cellophane sack of something to Jeremy. I could have reached out and touched her, but I never moved. She smelled unpleasantly of perfume and tobacco, both stale.

"Did I get any calls?"

Jeremy shook his head.

"I can't handle it," Tiffany said. "Mom home yet?"

Again Jeremy shook his head and pretended to press several keys on his machine.

"Awesome," she remarked. "Then I'm like the boss here, you know? Hey, look!" Her hand swept out to point at the broken window on Jeremy's machine, scattering the Dorito things all over. "You totaled your screen, you little airhead. Like don't even *consider* borrowing my Sony."

The very thought of anybody borrowing her . . . Sony seemed to turn Tiffany into a raging beast. She whirled my way and punched Darth Vader beside me. It hit the wall and bounced back. If she had another punch to deliver, I'd take it full in the face. Still, I never moved or even blinked.

"Like, aren't you a little old for dolls?" she sneered at Jeremy. "Ew, these are super skanky." She gestured at me and Darth. "Like Barf City. Gross me out. Totally."

"Just . . . get . . . outta . . . my room, Tiffany," Jeremy said hopelessly.

"Who needs you, honker?" Tiffany slumped from

the room and banged the door behind her. I'd never heard tell of a girl named for a lamp before, though this one was none too bright.

Jeremy wiped small beads of sweat off his forehead. He blinked at me like I might not come to life again. I blinked back, glad for the chance, and stepped out of my pose.

"That is one bad-tempered girl," I remarked. "What's put her in such a mean mood?"

"Tiffany?" Jeremy said. "Oh, that's as good as she gets. Basically I guess it's because we're from a broken home."

I scanned the room again. It looked all right to me. "The roof fell in on me and Mama once," I said. "And the porch has fallen off the house a couple times."

Jeremy stared. "Not that kind of broken home," he explained. "I mean our mom and dad don't live together anymore. Dad's living in a singles condo complex out on the Airport Highway."

"Oh, well, shoot," I responded. "I'm in a similar situation myself. The last time we saw my paw, he was hopping a freight for Centralia."

Jeremy poked his spectacles higher on his nose. "You mean in olden times you people had divorce?"

"Well, I don't know about divorce," I said. "That sounds expensive."

"I thought that all you did was pop corn and bake bread and sit around the fire telling stories and laughing a lot. It's on all the Christmas cards."

I decided not to try to explain to him about Mama.

*

I spent a restless night, though it gave me time to ponder. There were a couple of beds, one stacked upon the other. Jeremy sent me up a ladder to the top one. I was to sleep up there flat against the wall where nobody could see me.

I may have dozed, for I seemed to dream of pages fluttering off a calendar decorated with rocket ships. I dreamed, too, of Alexander Armsworth holding his lantern aloft in the immense distance. Waking once, I sensed some newcomer in the room. It must have been Jeremy's mama. Light from the hall slanted across the room, and a figure approached to check on him. But when she went away, she eased the door shut with care, so it couldn't have been Tiffany.

Toward morning I was awake again. "Jeremy?" I said quietly.

"Yes?" He was as awake as me.

"I've been giving this entire mess some thought. It couldn't have been the storm and your machines that brought me here. Not entirely. My particular Gift works in a different way. Seems like I'm drawn out of my time to those in need."

There was silence in the bed below.

"Do you follow this line of thought?" I inquired.

"Yes," he said. "Need. I'm going to need some replacement parts. The screen, of course, and all the circuitry governing the editing function and error detection. We're talking in the neighborhood of a couple hundred bucks over the warranty just to get even. But I can cover it."

I sighed. "If you're talking about your machines, Jeremy, that's not quite the kind of need I meant."

✻

Then, while I was resting my eyes, it was suddenly daylight in the room. A shock of red hair and two eyes appeared by my pillow. Jeremy hooked his spectacles over his ears and gave me more close looks. We were about nose to nose, but still he stared. He even studied Mama's old fur piece around my neck like it might be growing on me.

"You're still . . . here," he said quietly. "I guess we better consider your . . . bodily functions."

"Whoa!" says I. "Listen, where I come from we don't discuss that type thing in mixed company."

"Well, my bathroom's right through that door if you need it, and . . . do you eat?"

What did he take me for? I gave him a disgusted look, and he decided to check out the house, darting for the door in a pair of pajamas printed all over with moons and airships.

As I was climbing down the ladder from my socalled bed, Jeremy ran into his sister in the hall outside. I froze to hear her greet him in her rude way. She called him both nerd and honker and invited him to bag his face. Then she lumbered off down the stairs. The house rocked as Tiffany banged out the front door.

Jeremy popped back into the room. "The coast is clear," he announced. "I heard Mom's Trans Am tool out of the garage before I got up. She's an interior decorator."

Though this meant little to me, it seemed to calm him. "Come on," he said. "Let's find some breakfast."

I hung back, not scared exactly, but a little uncertain.

"It's okay," he said, but still, I was far from sure. He walked over to where I stood, digging my toe into the carpet. "Don't worry." A little shy himself, he put out a hand and took mine.

It was quiet then, but for the cheeping of a bird or two outside the window. *At least they haven't done away with birds,* I thought.

Jeremy peered at me in his thoughtful way. "I guess you'd be a real old lady now if you . . . I mean, you know what I mean."

I nodded. "I guess I'd be a real old lady or . . . out of the picture entirely." I pointed to the ceiling. In the mornings I tend to be moody.

"Well, anyway," said Jeremy, "come on. We can't hang around up here all day. I don't have a chance of sending you back till I can give my equipment a little TLC. We've got to go to school."

I hadn't thought of that.

"School? I'm a fugitive from 1914, Jeremy.

They'd drop a net over me and put me in a side-show!"

"Oh, just chill out on that, Blossom," he said. "I got that part all programmed. You can leave that to me."

So having little choice, I followed him out into his world, though my spirits were not high. There was more trouble ahead. It stood to reason.

12

As FAR AS I COULD SEE, every corner of the old Leverette farmhouse had been brought up-to-date. Though it was not to my taste, it was all strictly modern.

In my opinion, the kitchen went too far. It was one machine after another, each with its own name: Cuisinart and Frigidaire and Hotpoint and Whirlpool. It was all microwave this and radar control that.

I looked for the drainboard where Alexander was going to stretch out Champ Ferguson for a monster. In its place were big double sinks and a drain that chopped up the garbage and ate it.

When Jeremy showed me how this so-called garbage disposal worked, I remarked, "You don't leave much for the hogs."

He shook his head. "It's against the zoning to keep livestock in Bluffleigh Heights. I guess you people in the olden times kept a lot of hogs and chickens around."

"I have handled no hogs," I replied, "but I've kept a chicken or two."

We were to eat our breakfast on high stools
drawn up to a slick counter. Jeremy slid a bowl
before me. "This is basically a high-fiber whole-
grain product with dried fruit and wheat germ addi-
tives and minimal preservatives."

"It looks like fodder to me," I said suspiciously.
"What's fodder?"

"It's what you'd find in the nose bag of a horse," I
said. "Tastes like it, too."

We washed this mess down with a couple glasses
of what Jeremy called a vitamin C concentrate. I've
personally had better grub out of Mama's kitchen,
which is only a cookstove and a cupboard, basically.

The little clock on the counter flashed the time in
red numbers. Jeremy noticed and said, "Just stay
here, Blossom. I'll be right back. Then you'll see
how we're going to pull off going to school together.
It'll be a real scam. Trust me." He charged out of
the kitchen in his airship pajamas.

What could I do? I was a stranger in strange
parts. I sat waiting as the high-fiber whole-grain
product settled like a brick in the pit of my stomach.
The clever little so-called clock flashed 8:07, then
8:08.

I wondered how I was to pass unnoticed in Jeremy's magnet middle school. I thought of Daisy-Rae
holed up in her stall of the rest room and wondered
if that was a possibility for me. Away my mind
wandered.

It'd been a hard night, and my guard was down.
Maybe I heard a noise outside the house, maybe not.

Suddenly footsteps sounded on the back porch. I about jumped out of my skin and fell off the stool.

A key fumbled for the back door lock. There I sprawled in a heap on the kitchen floor, and in the wrong decade altogether. The key turned. I'd never make it to the dining room. There was a big double-door electrified icebox nearby. With any luck, I might squeeze in between it and the wall. I made one of my giant leaps.

Planting one boot in the little space, I was knocked nearly senseless by a collection of brooms and mops that keeled out on my head. There was hardly room for them, and none for me. When the kitchen door opened, I was standing right by it in full view.

A woman entered. She carried a ring of keys and a large paper bag of supplies. It hid her face from me and mine from her. She wore pants like a man and high-heeled shoes, which is one odd combination. Staggering under her load, she brushed past me.

I never moved, though I slewed my eyes around to the door. If I budged, she'd notice. But I might make a clean getaway. Still, I didn't like leaving the house on my own, never knowing what new threat might wait for me outside.

The woman eased her bag onto the counter and began taking various grocery items out of it. She had Jeremy's red hair, and I figured she was his mama. I was about to surrender myself to her and hope for the best, though it's always difficult to explain anything to a mother. I took one brave step forward and began to clear my throat.

At that moment she reached into her grocery bag and hefted out a cardboard container, labeled "LIGHTLY LUSCIOUS LOW-FAT MILK." She jerked open a door on the icebox, and it caught me square in the face. I slammed back into the corner by the brooms. My nose seemed mashed level with my cheeks, and it hurt too bad to cry.

The woman continued with her tasks, jamming various items into cupboards. She reached up and turned the knob of a small device sitting on a high shelf.

Though my nose was throbbing, I gaped in wonder. In the window of this gadget a tiny man appeared. The kitchen filled with the sound of his piping voice. It was some kind of improvement on the Bijou Picture Show moving pictures, with color and noise added. The cheerful little man on the screen was doing exercises to music, much as Miss Fuller operates in Girls' Gym. The midget man danced about like a cunning monkey. He had a head of hair as frizzy as my own.

"Well, now I've seen everything!" I exclaimed, but Jeremy's mama never heard me. Her hands were busy with her chores, and her eyes were glued on the little exercise man. But she was about to get a shock. And so was I.

A fearful figure entered from the dining room. Though the creature was not tall, it filled up the door from side to side. Its skin was silver, and its arms and legs were ringed like thick snakes. Its knees were large shiny circles, and its boots were of tremendous size. Something like a fishbowl served for its head. It grunted.

I was speechless, but Jeremy's mama took one look and let rip an almighty scream. In her hand had been a box labeled "FRUIT LOOPS." This object went soaring through the air, narrowly missing me.

Her hands clapped over her heart, and she slumped. "Oh, Jeremy," she said, "what are you doing in that thing, and why aren't you in school?"

His voice came from far off inside the fishbowl.

"Hi, Mom. We're wearing costumes today. It's the school Halloween party. I'm just leaving."

By squinting, I could make out his face blurred behind curved glass. It was Jeremy's voice, too, more or less. His eyes shifted to me, and he sized up the situation. I saw he was going to keep his mama talking while we got out of there somehow.

"Did Tiffany wear a costume to school?" she asked.

"Mom, you know those high school kids think they're too grown-up for that. Besides, Tiffany looks like Halloween all year long."

"Now, Jeremy." His mama sighed. "And what are you supposed to represent?" She planted a hand on her hip and examined his outfit.

"I'm a Citizen of the Galaxy, of course," Jeremy said in a hollow voice. "You're definitely not up on your Robert Heinlein, Mom. I made my knees out of hubcaps. What do you think?"

"They're . . . tubular. And what did you do with the goldfish?" she asked, staring him in the globe.

"They're in the powder room sink," he said, waving a kind of flipper. "They'll be fine."

His mama stood between us, but he still had her full attention. "If you don't scoot," she said, "you'll be late. Maybe I ought to drive you, but I've got six window treatments to finalize this morning and a designer sheet luncheon."

"No sweat," Jeremy said quickly, swinging his large legs and taking two steps toward me and the back door. "Plenty of time."

Not able to look back because of his glass head, Jeremy made steady strides. At the last moment he grabbed my hand, and we issued out the back door.

"Have a nice day, honey," his mama called out, absorbed once more in the little exercise man inside the moving picture box.

*

There were no sidewalks in Bluffleigh Heights, and all the paved streets curved, seeming to go nowhere. Me and Jeremy made our way along in the ditch while he learned to walk in his costume. He soon got the hang of it, throwing one padded leg around the other.

There'd been progress of a sort in automobiles. They had glass in all their windows now and strictly modern headlamps. They could get up high speeds, too, though many slowed at sight of me and Jeremy.

"I begin to see your scam," I told him as we

ambled on. "I'm to change into your Citizen of the
Galaxy outfit and wear it to school, as nobody will
see my face clear in that bowl. But what are you
going to wear?"

He blinked like a fish wearing spectacles.

"Actually," he said, "I'm going to wear this, and
. . . you're sort of in costume already. If you see
what I mean."

I looked down at myself: at Mama's old fur piece
with the fox face and bent ears. At my tarnished
spelling medal. At my old patched princess dress
that lapped down over my everyday boots. I saw
what he meant.

"What about my face?" I asked. "I don't have a
mask."

Even through the bowl, I met Jeremy's gaze. I
saw what he meant.

*

The way I figured it, a school is a school, throughout history.

But when Bluffleigh Heights Magnet Middle
School hove into view, I couldn't make head or tail
of it. It was a low, flat-roofed structure crouching in
a bald yard. There was no architecture to it. Miss
Mae Spaulding, principal of Horace Mann, wouldn't
have run a worm farm in the place. But the usual
crowd churned around outside, showing off. Most
were in Halloween costumes, though in the 1980s
it's hard to tell.

Jeremy began to drag his feet. The costume was a

burden to him, and his bowl was fogged up from heavy breathing. "This is the part I hate," he mumbled.

"If you're worried about me," I told him, "I can always nip down to the rest room for the day. This girl I know, name of Daisy-Rae, spends half her life in—"

He shook his bowl. "I didn't mean you. I'm glad you're here, Blossom. It's . . . just going to school I hate." His voice rang sorrowfully.

"That's only natural," I pointed out. "But shoot, Jeremy, you're a right bright kid—Gifted, I mean."

"It's not the schoolwork," he said faintly. "There's nothing to that. It's . . . everything else."

I should have known right then why I'd found my way through time to Jeremy. The evidence had been piling up from the first moment. But it was too simple to see.

Many in the crowd stared our way and laughed like hyenas. One girl was dressed up as a pig in a picture hat. She was the durnedest-looking thing I ever saw. Pointing right at me, she remarked at the top of her lungs that I was so grody she couldn't handle it.

As far as I could tell, we fitted right in. One of the boys had painted his face green and wore a cape with a stake through his heart. Some of them hardly wore enough to cover their shame, and I personally counted seven Darth Vaders. The smallest kid in the bunch, wearing a neat white suit, did nothing but run in circles, proclaiming, "Da plane come, boss. Da plane come."

It was a sight.

I'd decided to lay low and keep my mouth shut, always a good plan. But a rough type stepped into my path. "Awright," he barked. "Take off your mask, so we can like see who you are." He made a grab for my nose.

"Bag your face, honker," I replied with dignity.

This could have led to fisticuffs; but a bell rang within the so-called school, and we were carried along with the tide. Jeremy reminded me of Alexander Armsworth, as he was never a step ahead of me. I began to wonder who was looking after who. Through the schoolhouse doors we swept, though I personally had little hope for the place.

13

It was a madhouse all morning long, and little learning took place. Every class period was a Halloween party, though I doubt things were much better on a regular day. As for decoration, they had no orange and black crepe paper. Instead, all the walls were brightened up with a thing called graffiti, much of it poorly spelled.

Before the first class, which may have been English, I mumbled to Jeremy in alarm, "I'll be one too many when they take attendance."

"Take what?" Jeremy asked, and into the room we ganged. There was much milling around in there, and I swear to this day I never spied the teacher. If this was the Gifted bunch, may I never see the slow ones.

But I soon saw a sight all too familiar to me: a gang of stuck-up girls sitting in a tight clump. Remembering the Sunny Thoughts and Busy Fingers Sisterhood, I meant to give this bunch all the free air they could breathe. When I settled into a desk, Jeremy drifted away. This being eighth grade, everybody steered clear of the opposite sex.

One stuck-up girl spotted me at once. She was pretty to a fault and wore a ballerina costume with a sickeningly pink tutu. In her hand she carried a wand with a glittering little star at the end of it. She waved it around in sweeping gestures.

"Oh, you guys," she said to the girls, "like, look!" She waved her wand at me. "That is *so* grisly, like I am *sure*."

"Ew," said all her group, looking my way. "Gross us out," they said in a chorus.

"That is so *ill*," said the pig girl in the picture hat. "Gag me with a spoon. Really. Is that makeup or a mask? And what does the eighteen mean on her . . . hat?"

"Oh, I know what that means," said the ballerina, wielding her wand. "On an Ugly Scale of one to fifteen, she's an eighteen."

The whole group rocked with laughter, like they were supposed to.

I had the durnedest feeling I'd been through all this before.

"But who *is* she?" wondered the pig girl.

At that the ballerina, quick to take charge, jumped up and began counting the noses of her bunch with the wand: "Melissa, Kelly, April, Chrissy, Michelle, Hilary, Heidi." She sighed with relief. "*We're* all here." Then she flopped down, and the group closed ranks around her, losing all interest in me.

But I hadn't lost all interest in them. I edged out of my desk and made my way across the littered room to where they clustered like birds of bright plumage.

"Ew, get away," said several.

"Like, no way is she going to sit with us," said the pig person.

"For sure," came a chorus, and they all looked to the ballerina for leadership.

Arranging my fur piece, I marched up to her.

She tapped her wand nervously on the desk, as all eyes were upon her, including my beady black ones. "Say, sister," I said, "what's your name?"

They all gasped in shock.

"That's *Heather*," said several, amazed at my ignorance.

"Is that a fact?" I remarked, taking a closer look. I had the odd notion I knew her.

"You must be like really new in town. Really," breathed the pig. "Like a foreigner or something."

"Oh, no," I answered. "I'm an . . . old settler in these parts." I grinned at them in Mama's evil way. "Sort of the Spirit of Halloween Past." They shrank.

"In fact," I said, warming up, "I'm planning to tell fortunes and give readings and bring messages from various worlds to customers at a certain Halloween Festival . . . tomorrow night."

I had them listening now. But Heather drew in her cheeks and said, "I'm sure," in a mocking way.

"In fact, I feel one of my trances coming on right now." I swayed slightly and let my eyes roll back in my head like Mama does.

I had them in the palm of my hand now, though

many threatened to rolf on the floor. "Barf City," said the pig.

I swayed some more and let my long, bony finger reach out, drawing a bead on Heather's forehead.

"She is so zeeked out," said Heather uncertainly, "like, forget it, okay?"

By now my eyes were staring at the back of my skull. "*I have a message for a girl name of Heather that comes to her from the Great Beyond,*" I moaned in a truly hideous voice. "*This is your grandmother speaking, Heather, honey,*" I continued, squeaking like an old lady.

"I am *so* sure," Heather said to her group. "How could she know my family, she's so scruff. Besides, Grandma isn't in the Great Beyond. She's down in Sun City, Arizona."

"*It is I, Heather, honey,*" I squeaked hollowly, "*Grandma, down here in—ah—Sun City. Just wanted to say hello and . . . stay as sweet as you are, precious.*"

"Wig me out," said Heather, scratching at her little golden curls with her wand. "If you're so smart," she said to me, "what's my grandma's name?"

I had her there.

"*Why, Heather, honey,*" I answered in a real far-off voice, "*you know my name as well as your own. We were always one of the First Families of Bluff City. Silly child, I am the former* LETTY SHAMBAUGH."

Heather's wand clattered to the floor. "*Grandma!*" she shrieked, both wigging and zeeking right out. Even her tutu collapsed in a quivering pink mass.

As her group closed around her pale and trembling form, the pig girl rose up, shouting, "Somebody go for a guidance counselor for Heather!" The pig straightened her picture hat in a businesslike way, ready to assume command of the group.

I withdrew.

*

That was the only bright spot in a dismal morning. We moved from Halloween party to Halloween party, all at the taxpayers' expense. After my run-in with Heather's bunch nobody would come near me. Several whispered remarks, though, and pointed my way.

I noticed Jeremy wasn't doing much better. In every class there was a bunch of boys in a tighter clump than the girls. But Jeremy was never one of them.

He sat forlorn and friendless at a desk while the others entertained themselves by pouring Halloween punch from paper cups on one another. Occasionally one of them would come over to drum on Jeremy's bowl with a pencil. Otherwise, he seemed to be a perfect outcast.

I supposed Jeremy, being right smart, didn't fit in. The dumb ones always make the best followers. Still, he was one lonesome kid. I know the feeling.

By noon I was up to here with Bluffleigh Heights Magnet Middle School. We all were following an evil cooking smell to a place called the cafeteria when I remarked to Jeremy, "How's about you and me playing hooky?"

"Playing what?" he said, stumping along on his big silver legs.

"It's a rotten shame to waste the day in a place like this," I said. "Besides, I've got to start thinking about getting back you-know-where. Tonight's the night I'm to report to Old Man Leverette when those boys are going to make a mess of his front porch. I just naturally have to be there to teach—"

"Oh, I don't think you can get back that quick, Blossom." He spoke in a rush, like he didn't want me to go. "But we can cut out of school if you want to. How about checking out the mall? We could always cruise past Radio Shack and have a look at their components."

It didn't sound like my kind of place. We made a sharp turn just before the cafeteria and slipped outside through a fire door. A person couldn't hear herself think in that school.

"Now where?" Jeremy wondered.

"Bluff City." I spoke firmly. He reminded me of Daisy-Rae and Roderick. It was uphill work to get them into town, too. "There's got to be something left of the town I knew, and I mean to find it, Jeremy. I know curiosity killed the cat. But satisfaction brought that cat back."

"It's a long way," he said, "and this costume is pretty heavy."

I thought he might slip back home and change

into his regular clothes. I had no doubt he could pull this off, as his mama was not a noticing kind of woman. Besides, she'd be at her . . . designer sheet luncheon. But he pointed out that since I was going dressed as I was, he'd better stick to his costume.

Away we labored over the curving streets of Bluffleigh Heights on a brisk autumn afternoon seventy years hence.

Jeremy was a good companion, though mostly quiet inside his fogbound bowl. We walked for a quarter of an hour, and still I could see nothing familiar. It's a sight how homesick a person can get this near home.

What looked like pastureland in Old Man Leverette's south forty turned out to be something called the Little League field. When we came to where the old streetcar trestle spanned Snake Creek, there was only a wide highway bridge choked with automobiles speeding past a 7-Eleven store at the far end.

A lump was fast forming in my throat. Being a sensitive type, Jeremy noticed. His spectacles were steamed up, and his bowl was blurry; but he didn't miss much. "Tell me what it was like, Blossom. The olden days, I mean."

Since he seemed to know no history whatsoever, I told him various true stories.

One of them was how I happened to borrow a chicken from Old Man Leverette. That just naturally brought up the swimming hole in Leverette's Woods and how I chanced to observe Alexander

Armsworth and his cronies swimming and smoking in the altogether.

I went on to tell him about Mr. Ambrose Lacy, who had both Miss Spaulding and Miss Fuller on the string. I told him about Letty Shambaugh and her club and how Alexander took her to the moving pictures. And that brought up Daisy-Rae and Roderick. I worked in pretty nearly everybody.

I even mentioned how my mama's occult Powers had warned her of the old abandoned Leverette farmhouse and its eerie Vibrations.

"She was plugging into my malfunctioning electronic impulses," Jeremy observed. "There are people who can pick up shortwave radio on their hearing aids and false teeth. Your mom is probably a natural transistor."

"Wouldn't surprise me a bit," I said.

All this conversation carried us right into town. There beside a busy street was a sign that read:

WELCOME TO BLUFF CITY
68,002

"Sixty-eight thousand and two what?"

Jeremy blinked. "People."

"Well, I'll be a ring-tailed monkey!" I exclaimed.

On we went, deeper into this swollen Bluff City. Then, with minds of their own, my feet swerved away from the sidewalk. We took off across a vacant lot and down an alley.

Jeremy had to struggle along in his Galaxy boots

over ruts and a number of objects labeled NO
DEPOSIT, NO RETURN. "Where are we heading?"
He peered anxiously at the backs of various build-
ings.

"I'm switched if I know," I said. "It just feels
right."

It wasn't a minute more before I saw a familiar
sight against the sky. It was the roof and bell tower
of Horace Mann School. The bell tower was
boarded up, and there were missing shingles on the
roof; but my eyes misted over at sight of the old
place.

Dragging Jeremy along, I said, "Well, of course.
It's all crystal clear to me now. This route we've
been following down back alleys was once the
streetcar right-of-way. Many's the time I've walked
the rails along here."

Grunting to keep up, Jeremy followed my skip-
ping form into the old schoolyard.

"And here's where we had our graduation day
maypole dance last—"

A sign above the schoolhouse door caught my
eye. It was a new one, and it read:

MAE SPAULDING MEMORIAL
MEDIA CENTER

Substance Abuse Counseling Available

I blinked. This was more information than I
could . . . program. Instead, I grabbed Jeremy's
puffy sleeve. "And right across the road is Bluff City
High—"

But across the paved street was no such thing. My old high school had been leveled. In its place was a large, rude structure topped by a gaudy sign:

INTOWN MOTEL
* DAY RATES * WATER BEDS * CABLE TV *
* ICE MACHINES *

My heart sank. They had erased my world.

14

A MOMENT PASSED before I felt Jeremy's hand patting my arm.

"I'm sorry, Blossom." He spoke in a small, kindly voice.

"What happened to my world? There's nothing left. It just as well never have existed."

"It's a . . . rotten shame," he said.

"I'm grossed out, Jeremy," I whimpered.

But it's always darkest before the dawn, as I've often said. I gathered up my courage, ready to scout out more hopeful landmarks than these.

> "There is nothing either good or bad,
>   but thinking makes it so,"

I said to him.

"That's a good attitude," Jeremy remarked.

"It's *Hamlet*. Act Two."

On we went where the streetcar tracks had been until we came to a paved yard with rows of little mechanical hitching posts. A sign read:

METERED PARKING

I knew where we were now. Our path was crossing Fairview Avenue, the proud street lined with the all-brick homes of the well-to-do. "Letty Shambaugh lived in that very house." I pointed to the large and tasteful residence.

But her porch had been hacked off. A shutter or two hung from a single hinge. The houses on either side were gone, like missing teeth. "Must have been a fire," I remarked.

"Several," Jeremy said. "This neighborhood hasn't hit bottom yet, but it's on the way down."

Overshadowing the entire street was a tremendous building with blank sides and skylights in the roof. We detoured from our path to read a sign over the entrance:

FULLER MEMORIAL RECREATIONAL
FACILITY
* JOGGING TRACK * HANDBALL COURTS *
* SENSIBLE WEIGHT REDUCTION *
* INTERPRETIVE DANCE *

"Eureka!" I exclaimed, smacking my forehead. "Don't you get it, Jeremy?"

He didn't seem to.

"This here recreational facility is named in memory of Miss Fuller, the Girls' Gym teacher. It's bound to be!"

Jeremy rubbed the bowl near his chin.

"And that media center back yonder is named in memory of Miss Spaulding."

Jeremy nodded.

"*Miss* Spaulding," I explained, "and *Miss* Fuller. They kept their maiden names right to the grave!"

"And that was good?" he pondered.

"Shoot, yes. It means that neither one of them fell into the clutches of Mr. Ambrose Lacy and married that two-timing polecat."

"Oh."

"I bet you *I* had something to do with that." I grinned evilly. "In fact, I ought to be getting back to 1914 this very minute, and—"

"Come on, Blossom." Jeremy caught up my hand and pulled me along back toward the streetcar right-of-way. "Let's see some more. This is interesting. Really."

And of course it was. And about to get more so.

As we threaded our way along through the alleys, I knew we'd soon come to the place where me and Mama lived. Jeremy knew, too, as I'd told him how me and her occupied a property hard by the tracks right behind Alexander Armsworth's barn.

As we trudged along, Jeremy said, "You won't be too disappointed if—"

"Not me. Our place was fixing to fall down even back then. If Letty's big house hasn't held up, I can't expect too much from our old dump."

Which was just as well. When we came to the home of my youth, there was nothing there but smoothly mowed grass and a tremendous big horse tank with soft sides of a bright blue color. It was brimming with water, but not a horse in sight.

"Well, that's where me and Mama lived," I said, just lightly stroking her fur piece. "But what in the Sam Hill do you call that big soft horse tank?"

"That's an aboveground swimming pool," Jeremy said. "But look, Blossom, that barn you told me about is still here."

And so it was. I chanced a look at it from the corner of my eye. The barn on the old Armsworth property stood where it always had, in good repair, too.

I shrank then and felt the chill winds of autumn around my heart. Oh, I didn't fear that barn because it had once been haunted. It wasn't the past that worried me. It was this future.

His globe glancing everywhere, Jeremy waddled to the far side of the barn while I remained rooted to the spot. He waved a padded arm for me to follow, but I wouldn't. I still felt the chill.

Presently I saw his silver form returning around the corner of the barn. "It's still there, Blossom," he said, loud inside his bowl. "A great big old house with fancy porches and turrets and a lot of colored glass over the doors. It's nice."

"Well," I said thoughtfully, "it was always one of the better addresses."

"And guess what, Blossom. It's still being lived in. They haven't turned it into a media center or a recreational facility or a free clinic or anything. There are curtains at all the windows and pots of flowers on the sills. There's a power mower on the lawn, and they've even got all their leaves bagged. There's a Buick Century in the driveway. Come on, let's check the place out. We can always pull the old trick-or-treat number on them." Jeremy bounced in his space boots and reached for my hand.

But I drew it back.

I thought of the Armsworth mansion as I'd known it. I smelled bacon frying and thought of the Armsworths having their breakfast every morning as I made my way to school across their property. I thought of Alexander Armsworth. And not just as the kid I'd known. I thought of myself, too, as I was and as I would be.

"No, Jeremy," I said. "I better not find out who those people are up in the house now. There's some things about the future a person ought not to know. I think we should turn back now."

"Back?" Jeremy said faintly. His hand was still out for mine.

"Back to Bluffleigh Heights, and then I think we better say our good-byes."

There was a small lump in my throat, for many reasons, and a small lump in Jeremy's, too. I noticed it just under the rim of his bowl.

15

We had no trouble getting past Jeremy's mama and back up to his room. It was just evening, and we had the shadowy upstairs to ourselves. Tiffany wasn't home. The mall hadn't closed.

The dark corners made the place more like the old abandoned Leverette farmhouse. Once in his room with the door closed behind us, Jeremy reached for the light switch, but I drew his hand away.

"I might get back better in the dark," I said.

He turned away from me and eased the fishbowl off his head. "Oh, wow. I'm glad to get out of that thing. I guess this is about my last year for Halloween, the costume part at least."

His head of hair was faintly red in the failing light. It stood up in peaks. He slipped off his hubcaps and massaged his knees. Then he took off his spectacles and breathed on them. He was only playing for time.

"I've had a real nice visit, Jeremy. Many thanks."

"My pleasure," he said politely. I reckon his voice

was changing, for it cracked then. "Come back any . . . time."

"Well, I don't know about that," I said. "But I guess I can figure how I happened to pay this particular call."

"There were the electrical storms," he said, "one at my end and one at—"

"I doubt it was the weather, Jeremy. I figure maybe you needed a friend."

He wasn't sure. "Looks like you came a really long way just to spend a little time with me."

"Well, there's nothing more important than friendship," I said. "I get a little lonesome now and again myself. Maybe I came for us both."

"Seems like you just got here, and now you're leaving."

"Well, that's me all over," I told him. "Busy every minute. Tonight I'll be at Old Man Leverette's town residence, teaching Alexander's bunch a lesson. Then tomorrow night I'll be right here in this very house, telling fortunes.

"Did I tell you we of the freshman class are running your place as a Haunted House? We're going to stretch Champ Ferguson out on the drainboard as a monster and run a crackerjack dungeon and model torture chamber in your cellar. We're going to have ghosts in your corners and bats in your belfry. We're going to charge ten cents."

"It sounds great," Jeremy said with his head down. "Wish I could come along."

But he couldn't, and he knew it.

"You can be there in . . . spirit," I said. "You can think of us tomorrow night seventy years ago. I could even tell my fortunes right here in your room. Shall I?"

He nodded. His eyes were glistening. Maybe mine were, too.

"Blossom, since you've got to be going, I guess I can tell you this." Jeremy rubbed one of his padded legs with his big boot. "I haven't had too much experience with knowing girls. But I really like you, a lot. Of course, you're . . . different."

"Oh, well, shoot," I said, my face a little warm, "I've been called different even in my own time."

Jeremy smiled a little and scratched his red thatch. "I guess what I'm trying to say is, if I was Alexander Armsworth, it wouldn't be Letty Shambaugh I was taking to the . . . moving pictures."

The last light left the room then. There was nobody to see, and with any luck I'd soon be gone. So I thought: *Oh, well, shoot.* Then I stepped forward and gave Jeremy a little kiss good-bye.

He took it real well. Then he said, "Blossom, when you're gone, how will I know you were ever really here? I see you're real now, but later I might wonder."

"Like I was only a stage you were going through?" I asked him. "And later you outgrew it?"

"Like that," he said, "basically."

I chanced to glance down at my spelling medal then. It was hanging by a thread from Mama's old ratty coat. I'd sworn to wear that medal till it fell off me. I gave it a little tug, and it came loose in my hand.

"Here." I held it out to him. "I was the champion speller of Horace Mann School. This medal was at one time my most prized possession. Take it to remember me by. It will always remind you that you have a friend, a good old friend."

Jeremy reached out and pulled back. "Tell you what, Blossom. Take it along with you on your trip and hide it somewhere in this house, somewhere I can find it later on if I begin to forget. Sometime when I'm lonesome again, like I was before you came."

"Let me see," I pondered. "Where'd be a place safe for seventy years?" Then it came to me. "You know that china closet down in your dining room? Roderick hid in there one time and liked to scare the wits out of Alexander Armsworth, though it didn't faze me."

"China closet?" Jeremy said. "Oh, yes, we keep the stereo components in there."

"First time you get lonesome, check around in there. You'll find this spelling medal of mine under a loose floorboard. That'll be a sign I'm thinking of you."

"Is there a loose floorboard?"

"There will be."

It was time to go then, and we both knew it.

Jeremy drifted over to his machines. They looked dead as doornails to me, and I don't suppose he could get a beep out of them. But he said, "I could try a little patching and looping to . . . help you off the launching pad."

But I told him I'd better try to do it my way. It was almost night then, and we were two dark shapes in the room—three if you count Darth Vader. I fastened my beanie tight with the hatpin and arranged Mama's fur piece so it wouldn't strangle me if I got up speed.

"This is the part I'm never sure about," I admitted. "I have to give it my all."

It grew darker then, dark as a pocket. I heard a distant sighing sound. It was the wind pump out past the chicken coop on the old abandoned Leverette farm. I cocked my ears to hear it clearer and let my brain go blank. I commenced to Vibrate, and I felt my mysterious Powers take charge.

Wind blew through Jeremy's window, for there was no glass in it now. A whirlwind circled my form and gave me goosebumps. There was a shower of sparks, but cold and white as snow. Or maybe these were the white pages torn from seventy calendars. Whatever they were, they gusted into a tremendous cyclone.

I never moved, and I traveled like the wind.

*

It was a gentle landing as these things go. There was no carpet on the floor now. The heels of my boots bumped on bare boards. They were gritty with plaster dust.

I'd kept my eyes tight shut, though not from fear exactly. When I looked around me, I was in the empty, ruined upstairs room of the old abandoned Leverette farmhouse. Pale moonlight fell through the broken window. My spelling medal was in my hand.

I walked toward the moonlight right through the emptiness where Jeremy's machines had been— would be. Torn wallpaper hung down in curls, and I smelled the smells of an empty old house far from town: the mildew and wood rot and dead field mice in the walls.

I chanced a look out the window. There I saw the black branches of Leverette's Woods beyond the gate to Lovers' Lane. The wind pump was back too, singing and turning in the night breeze. There was the chicken coop, right where it should be. In one of its windows was a coal oil lamp. The lamp burned low, for it was past Roderick's bedtime.

I looked for the blanket of glittering lights as far as the eye could see. I looked for the golden arches and "40 BILLION SOLD." But they weren't there, not yet. It was the night before Halloween. And it was 1914. My next thought was of Mama.

I cut and ran for home.

*

"Girl, where you bin?"
Before I could get across the threshold, she came

down on me like the Johnstown flood. I was out of breath from . . . much traveling, and I sagged somewhat in the doorframe.

Mama's teeth were out, but she was speaking clear. "You was gone all night and all day, too! I'll larn youoph."

She reached for Paw's razor strop that hangs over the pitcher and bowl. She saves this back for special occasions. Believe it or not, I was glad to see her.

"Well, Mama," I said, hoping to distract her, "have you had your supper?"

"Of course I ain't! And I see you come back empty-handed. I couldn't eat a bite anyhow." At least she seemed to forget the strop. The dice dangling down from her ears danced, and her flinty eyes bored into me.

"Why, Mama, I think you were worried about me," I said, pushing my luck.

"Worried you wouldn't come back?" she asked. "Or worried you would!"

She regarded me slyly. "Where you bin anyhow? You look like three sheets to the wind and somethun the cat drug in."

Still, I hoped to distract her. "I'm half-starved myself," I remarked. "I haven't had a thing to eat all day but whole-grain high-fiber product and a chaser of vitamin C concentrate."

"Talk sense," Mama said.

She dragged me to the table and dropped me in a chair. When she turned up the flame on the lamp, its reflection flared in her crystal ball.

"Now then." She settled into a chair opposite. "I asked where you bin one time. I won't ask agin." She pointed at Paw's strop. "I'll let that thing do the talkin'."

"Much as I'd like to chew the fat with you all evening, Mama, I have a busy night ahead of me and no time."

She squinted at me over the crystal ball. "You got all the time I say you got." Reaching into her shroud, she pulled out a plug of Bull Durham and commenced to jaw it at her leisure. "Start at the beginnin'."

"Well . . . it's like this, Mama. Last night I nipped back to the high school to get some homework I'd left in my desk. And lo and behold, if the janitor didn't come along and lock up all the doors! I was stuck in that high school all night, Mama. Why, I had to sleep under Miss Blankenship's desk. I overslept as it turned out, and the first thing I knew, it was morning. Miss Blankenship was taking attendance! So of course, all I could do was go through the regular school day as usual. That's about what happened . . . basically."

There was a disturbing pause before Mama said, "That ain't even close." She made a point of staring into her crystal ball like she could read the truth in it. "Try agin."

I fetched up a sigh. It's always difficult to explain anything to a mother, as I've often said. "The truth is, Mama, I did something you told me not to do."

"That don't come as a shock to me," she remarked, drumming her long fingers on Paw's strop.

"I went out to the old abandoned Leverette farmhouse last night."

Mama's eyes flashed, but she looked deep into her crystal ball. "And what did you find out?" she said cautiously. She was staring hard at the ball, but she was seeing nothing. She was all ears.

I thought of a way to flatter her somewhat. "I found out you were right, Mama. Remember that time you went into one of your trances and said, 'Not all the Unliving are dead'? You hit the nail on the head that time."

Mama folded her arms across her front and made a satisfied sound. "I'm never wrong," she remarked. "What did I mean exactly?"

"You meant that while some of the Unliving are dead, the rest of the Unliving haven't been born yet. They're the people of the future."

Mama gave this some thought. "That's real interesting, ain't it? Them trances of mine is a marvel. I don't know how I do it."

"Me either, Mama. When it comes to Powers, you don't know your own strength."

Mama almost beamed. I figured this was as good a time as any to make my exit. "However, even with my puny Powers," I told her, "I can read your mind this minute."

She froze. "Git outta my head, girl."

"Oh, yes, Mama, I read you like a book. You just

as well hand over that gunnysack at your feet. You know yourself you're fixing to send me out into the night to borrow a nice, plump frying chicken."

Mama looked uncertain, but hungry. She could all but smell that chicken frying now, though she had unfinished business with me.

I had unfinished business with her, too. If she lived to be a hundred, she'd never tell me how strong her Powers are. She'd half known the old abandoned Leverette farmhouse was haunted by the future, so to speak. But I bet you a nickel my Powers are stronger. I can't picture Mama traveling through a time warp. Not to mention what they'd think of her if she turned up in Bluffleigh Heights. I am no oil painting, but Mama would scare a bulldog off a meat wagon.

Mama had stood at the door of the Dreadful Future. There was no doubt in my mind about that. But I had crossed the fatal threshold!

She fished up the sack and scooted it across the table to me. When I reached out for it, I palmed her set of false teeth that were resting by the crystal ball. I slipped her teeth into my pocket and said, "I'll be off now to pay a call on Old Man L—"

"*Hush yore mouth,*" Mama commanded. "Don't *never* tell me where you git them chickens. What I don't know won't hurt me!"

"Oh, Mama." I sighed. "I'm glad you said that." Then I hightailed it out into the night.

16

IF YOU'D BEEN LINGERING around outside Old Man Leverette's house in Bluff City on the night of October 30, 1914, you could have seen it all for yourself. Delayed by Mama somewhat, I wasn't there a moment too soon, but a slicker operation was never pulled off.

Though I'm not used to approaching that particular house from the front, I slipped like a shadow across the Leverette yard, swerved around a sugar maple tree that shades his porch, and nipped up to his parlor door. I rapped but once before the door opened, and Old Man Leverette let me in. I've rarely, if ever, seen him in a better mood.

Minutes later both me and him reappeared on the porch. My form was draped in various white bed sheets. My head was bound up in a pillow slip that fitted tight across my forehead and flapped behind.

My face was a work of art. Old Man Leverette had smeared my cheeks and chin with lampblack and a coating of goose grease to make my entire face shine like a raw wound. Under my eyes he'd painted ghastly circles and bags with a red vegetable dye he'd prepared especially. I was Barf City.

In my hand I carried a red railroad lantern with the wick turned low. Under his arm Old Man Leverette carried a stepladder. He was chuckling and snorting in advance, worse than a kid himself.

"If we don't show them boys a thing or two," he wheezed, "you can call me a—"

"Never mind about that, Old—Mr. Leverette," I replied, all business. "Just steady that ladder and help me up that maple tree." Which he did.

I heard the ladder close below me and Old Man Leverette's heavy footsteps as he tramped back up on the porch and into the house.

The last leaf had fallen from the sugar maple, and its branches were slick with the evening damp. I needed to find just the right limb.

Flailing around in the tree like a big bird, I was hampered by my sheets. A limb overhung the front steps, but it was puny. I'd fallen out of one tree lately and didn't wish to make a habit of it. I eased into the gutter and rested from my climb. It was dark that night and chilly up there on the porch roof.

Turning up my lantern, I spied a stouter limb. It too branched out over the front steps. Throwing caution to the winds, I stood up in the gutter. Without looking down at certain doom or a broken leg at least, I flexed my knees and took the leap.

The lantern swinging from my elbow threw weird shadows across the yard. I hooked the stout limb with an arm and a leg and hung there swaying. Then I pulled myself up to a sitting position. I might have been a large white owl gone to roost up among the bare branches.

I practiced my gymnastics then, arranging the folds in my sheets so they wouldn't trip me up. I meant to put on a ghastly show, but I didn't plan to hang myself into the bargain. As it happened, I had little time to practice. From down the unpaved street I heard the unstealthy footsteps of boys. Three boys.

From my high perch I saw these shadowy three scramble off the crown of the road and skulk along in the weedy ditch. Though I couldn't make them out, I figured Champ and Bub were the front ones and Alexander was bringing up the rear. My lantern burned low.

When they came even with the fence by the Leverette property, they bent double and skulked for the house. Through the pickets I watched these three toad forms moving up toward the porch.

They cut around then for the steps and were soon in a bunch right beneath my dangling feet. They were punching each other and snorting with laughter, which they muffled with their sleeves. I got a strong whiff of horse manure.

They eased onto the porch, crab-fashion. "Who brought the matches?" I heard Alexander ask. He can't ever plan anything since he never thinks a minute ahead.

I couldn't see them then because they were work-

ing up by the front door. Bub doubtless planted the
paper sack of manure on the porch floor. Champ
doubtless brought the match I heard struck. Alexander doubtless rang Old Man Leverette's doorbell.

"Trick or treat!" Alexander cried out in a breaking voice.

"Oh, shut up," Bub said. Then they must have set
the sack afire, for the porch glowed.

Now was the moment when Old Man Leverette
was supposed to jerk open the door, see a small fire
on his porch, and jump on it to stamp it out. The
boys were poised for flight the second they saw that
front door begin to move.

They never saw it. While up above I hooked my
legs around the branch, Old Man Leverette
wrenched his front door open with lightning speed.
Never setting a foot outside, he swung his shotgun
just over the three boys' heads and let fly with both
barrels.

Rock salt raked the porch ceiling and pounded in
a hailstorm on the porch floor. The explosion was
heard downtown. It was like the Day of Judgment,
only louder.

This was followed by a piercing shriek which
could only be Alexander. When they could move,
Bub dived one way over the side of the porch, and
Champ dived the other. They both vaulted over a
matching pair of lilac bushes and lit, running.

There was a scuffling sound as Alexander's boots
seemed to run into each other. Then he turned and

plunged down the front steps, just as he was meant to do.

At the last possible moment, I popped Mama's false teeth into my mouth. Being too big for my head, they made a wonderful show. With all my might I swung forward on my branch.

Just as Alexander hit the porch steps in wild retreat, my deathly face, upside down, swung level with his. I held the lantern, turned up full blast. It lit my awful black and red features. Mama's terrible teeth grinned at him, and that is some sight. The night breeze caught my drapings. I was a floating head, and my sheets were the shroud from some troubled tomb.

It stopped Alexander cold. He couldn't see my knees hooked over the branch above him. He could see only a face with the features upside down in red shadow, hanging inches before him.

A pitiful gurgling sound formed in his throat. His elbows were tucked up at his sides for running, but he was paralyzed. His face seemed to dissolve. He spun around in panic and pounded back up on the porch. Which was another mistake.

Old Man Leverette had doused the small fire with a bucket of water he had ready. Now he'd picked up the paper sack which had burned down to the manure. In both hands the old gentleman hefted up the soggy sack.

Alexander ran straight into it, face first.

17

HALLOWEEN DAY dawned bright and fair, Indian summer as such weather is called. All the thoughts of us freshmen were upon the Halloween Festival Haunted House. Especially mine. But it was still a school day.

In homeroom Miss Blankenship took attendance as usual. Her daily *Hamlet* quotation was already on the blackboard:

I MUST BE CRUEL, ONLY TO BE KIND
Act III

We all sat restless in our rows, with scrubbed and shiny faces. Alexander Armsworth's face looked especially scrubbed.

But he wasn't sure whether he was speaking to me or not. I could read his mind like a book as he sat in the desk ahead of me. His ears glowed pinkish. Like Mama, he had some inkling of the mystery in the old abandoned Leverette farmhouse. But where I'd gone night before last when I'd walked through that fatal door, he couldn't be sure.

He also wasn't positive that it was me who was the ghastly floating red and black head which had caused him so much fear and discomfort last night. Hamlet himself had no more trouble making up his mind than Alexander.

But his ears were glowing redder. Just as the bell rang, ending homeroom, bells seemed to ring in Alexander's brain. He turned on me, hissing.

"Listen, Blossom, if I find out it was you last night you-know-where who made me get hit in the face with you-know-what, I will make you one sorry girl."

I looked back at him with wide and innocent eyes. But it didn't work. The bell had rung, and so I gathered up my schoolbooks and twitched up the aisle in Letty Shambaugh's way.

Alexander had not cooled off by history class. Long before the day was over, he had me tried and convicted in his mind.

"Listen," he hissed again, right under Mr. Lacy's nose, "you might as well come clean, Blossom. It was you up that tree because who else would pull such a disgusting stunt, you little—"

"Chill out, Alexander," I whispered sternly. "You had better keep your accusations to yourself until after tonight at least. That is, if you want any fortunes told in your so-called Haunted House."

This didn't calm him down, but it shut him up. "We have the reputation of the freshman class to consider," I added, sniffing.

All in all, it wasn't one of Alexander's better days. For one thing, he'd lost his freshman beanie someplace and didn't know where to find it.

I had it. Last night, when he'd received a faceful from Old Man Leverette, his beanie had shot off the back of his head, rolled down the porch steps, and come to rest under my dangling head. In the confusion that followed, Alexander had sped away, blind into the night.

I'd gathered up his beanie along with a plump fryer, cut up and ready for the pan, which Old Man Leverette gave me to remember the occasion by. Mama had made quick work of the chicken, but I still had Alexander's beanie. In such a mood as his, I didn't figure he deserved to have it back.

Mostly to hush us up, Mr. Lacy sent me down to the office with the attendance slip. As usual, I detoured past the girls' rest room to drop in on Daisy-Rae. Seemed like ages since I'd seen her last.

Much to my surprise, I found her out in the open, staring through the barred window by the sinks. You can't see anything through that window since it's frosted for modesty's sake. But Daisy-Rae's long face was turned to the sunlight filtering in.

"Hey, Blossom." She turned slowly to me.

"Hey, Daisy-Rae. Looks like you're getting braver." I gestured at the stalls. All of their doors were standing open.

"The sun felt so warm on my face," she said, mournful as a coot, "and I wasn't gittin' enough exercise in that place." She flapped a bony hand at her favorite stall. "Anyhow, I bin thinkin' about givin' up this whole education idea. Roderick is gittin' to where he can find his way to Horace Mann school by hisself."

I sighed. It seemed like everybody was in a glum mood today. I wondered how we'd get up enough freshman class spirit to run a crackerjack Haunted House tonight.

Right then something began to dawn on me. I don't know if I Vibrated or not, but somehow the sight of doleful Daisy-Rae slumped there by the sinks sent me a signal. I racked my brain, but I couldn't quite think it through. Then the light began to dawn.

"Say, Daisy-Rae, you coming to the Haunted House tonight?"

"Well, you'ens is havin' it right out by our place. I expect Roderick will want to go. You know how he is. But we ain't got ten cents between us. Kin you git us in?"

"Oh, shoot, Daisy-Rae, you won't have to pay. I have an idea we might need you'ens—you and Roderick to help us run the place."

She drew back. "Well, I'm not rilly a freshman," she said, "and I cain't picture Roderick ever bein' a freshman, so I don't think it'd be our place to take part."

"Daisy-Rae," I declared, "you are one shrinking violet. Just make sure you and Roderick are available tonight, as I think you two might come in real handy."

I left her drooped by the sinks, but she was look-ing as interested as she gets.

*

Mama watched me like a hawk as I flitted around our place getting ready for the Haunted House. She'd been casting spells to while away the time. But she pushed aside all her little sacks of garlic and wolfbane and suchlike and took up a pack of cards.

"Looks to me like if they'd wanted a *real* fortune-teller, they'd have had me," she remarked.

"Well, Mama, you are not a freshman."

She sent a jet of tobacco juice onto the floor.

"Can I wear this?" I asked her, holding up her old purple washable velveteen shawl with the gold fringe. I'd already talked her out of a pair of hoop earrings for the evening and a black sateen skirt which she'd sewed silver moons and stars all over.

As if by chance, I slipped my hand into one of the many pockets of this skirt and drew out her set of false teeth.

"Why, looky here, Mama. You have stuck your teeth in the pocket of this skirt. You're getting awful forgetful and liable to leave them around most any-place."

Her eyes flashed and narrowed. "Gimme them things." She slammed her teeth down on the table. "I bin lookin' for them high and low," she grumbled.

I flitted away, seeming to busy myself. But I soon flitted back. Mama had just turned up the queen of spades, one of her favorite cards.

"Girl, what you know about tellin' fortunes I could put in my ear and still have room for my elbow."

"Well, Mama, I'm willing to learn if you have any pointers for me."

"It takes talent," she said, studying the cards, "which you ain't got."

"I'd hoped to make a good showing," I said, "as it might send some business your way."

Mama brightened somewhat. Her hand hesitated over the jack of hearts.

"There'll be grown-ups at the Haunted House," I observed, "with money to spend. As a matter of fact, one of the chaperons for the occasion is Mr. Lacy, the history teacher."

Mama grunted.

"Mr. Ambrose Lacy," I said.

"Who?"

"You heard me, Mama. I told you all about how Mr. Lacy was sparking both Miss Spaulding and Miss Fuller at the same time. You said Ambrose Lacy was trouble with a capital *T* and always had been. You said you knew him."

The jack of hearts seemed stuck to Mama's hand. She raised the card to her forehead and closed her eyes, seeming to receive messages.

"Ambrose Lacy," she said in a distant voice. "Ah, yes, here comes Wisdom from the Great Beyond. Lay it on me!"

There's nobody like Mama for pretending to receive a message she's known all along.

"I see in my mind's eye a young squirt down in Sikeston, Missouri, where we all come from. There is bad blood there, and bad blood will out! I see this young punk, name of Ambrose Lacy, bein' shot at by a local farmer for foolin' with his wife. And then along about 1905 or 1906 I see Ambrose Lacy gittin' married to the daughter of a prominent feed and grain dealer. Oh, yeah, I see everything."

"Married!" I muttered.

"That's right," Mama said. "This philandering dude married the former Blanche Potts in one of them two years."

"Well, I never," I declared.

"It gits worse," Mama said, her eyes tight shut. "I see a little stranger in their midst. A small son born to this mismatched pair."

"A small son," I breathed in outrage.

"You heard me," Mama said.

"What's the kid's name, Mama? Think!"

She flattened the jack of hearts against her forehead. "Leonard," she said.

"Leonard?"

"Leonard. And before this youngen was weaned, his hardhearted papa—I'm talkin' about Ambrose Lacy—deserted wife and child and skipped town. He hasn't bin heard of in them parts since."

The jack of hearts fluttered from Mama's hand. Her eyes opened and gazed into mine. "That any use to you?" she said in a voice normal to her.

"I wouldn't be a bit surprised, Mama." I tucked her shawl around me, ready to be gone.

She scooped up her cards. "You better take this deck with you, and the crystal ball, too. With yore puny Powers, you'll need all the help you kin git."

"Many thanks, Mama."

When I reached for the deck of cards, her hand closed over mine. I thought she meant to read my palm, but she only gave my hand a little squeeze. There is no charting Mama's moods.

Wedging the crystal ball under my arm, I vanished out into the night, my hoop earrings swinging free.

18

CLOUDS RACED BEFORE THE MOON, and the old abandoned Leverette farmhouse stood tall against the night sky. I was about tuckered out from walking every step of the way from town burdened by the crystal ball. There was a touch of winter in the wind that gusted right through Mama's shawl.

The old house glowed, though not with electric light. An eerie candle burned in every window, planted there by freshman hands. Grinning jack-o'-lanterns flanked the front door.

Lingering in the tall weeds, I thought of Jeremy-to-be. I strained to hear a distant *beep* or possibly a *pyong*. But I only heard the wind pump humming its familiar song. I stood there a moment between worlds and thought of how much time there is, and how little.

A large Packard touring car advanced up the lane, raising a cloud of dust and chaff. It drew up with a flourish before the broken steps of the farmhouse. Letty Shambaugh with all her club tumbled out of the auto and ganged into the house under the sign that read:

REPENT WHAT'S PAST; AVOID WHAT IS TO COME

I had no doubt the boys were already inside the house, stretching Champ out on the drainboard and arranging the deadman's guts in the dungeon.

I hurried on, but not into the house just yet. Detouring around it, I made for the chicken coop. Except for details, my plan for drawing Daisy-Rae and Roderick into this evening's events was all but worked out. Without consulting the crystal ball, I foresaw a busy and productive evening for us all.

*

By nine o'clock the old abandoned Leverette farmhouse was full of customers. Letty's committee manned the door to relieve one and all of the dime admission.

Garbed as ghosts, various freshmen led the unsuspecting to where Harriet Hochhuth in a trick harness was hanging from a fake noose in the china closet. The guided tour included everything from the attic, where Tess and Bess Beasley cavorted as twin bats, to the monster's kitchen and the deadman's dungeon and model torture chamber. The place was a regular beehive, and we were minting money. Even sophomores, juniors, and seniors had drifted over from their fund raisers to take a trip through ours.

I sat at a table in an upstairs room, Jeremy's room. Before me were the crystal ball, the pack of cards, and a guttering candle. Screening the broken plaster walls were several sheets draped to suggest the mystery of a Gypsy's tent.

Above the entrance was a hand-lettered sign clearly thought up by Alexander:

FOR A NICKEL EXTRA, MADAME BLOSSOM TELLS ALL

Beneath this corn-fed sign I was at my post, wrapped in Mama's shawl, with a trick or two up my sleeve. Business was slow, but it was bound to pick up.

My first so-called customer was Letty Shambaugh, who popped in early to snoop. Big Maisie Markham was with her, since Letty doesn't like to face me alone.

The sight of both of them gave me a start. Maisie was costumed as Cleopatra, queen of Ancient Egypt. She wore enormous bloomers tied tight with silken cords around her thick ankles. A bejeweled jacket strained around her form and showed her middle. A chain of gold coins festooned her forehead. Embedded in the folds of her fat arm was a fake snake. She looked like three Cleopatras, all struggling for the throne.

Letty was tricked out as the new moving picture star Theda Bara of Hollywood. Her face was powdered dead white with arching eyebrows and a black rosebud where her mouth had been. She was all in clinging black taffeta with a Spanish mantilla of silk cobwebs and artificial spiders.

I seemed to think of another girl of my acquaintance—a certain ballerina wielding her wand.

"Well, Blossom," says Letty, planting her little hand on her hip, "we are doing a land office business elsewhere in this Haunted House, while here you sit all by your lonesome. But never let it be said that the freshman class didn't give you your chance."

"That's right," said Maisie.

I shuffled my deck. "Which one of you . . . ladies wants to be first?" I inquired.

"First what?" Letty elbowed Maisie out of the way.

"First to have a reading," I remarked, laying out the cards.

Letty shrank somewhat. "Your job is to fool the public, Blossom, not us."

My gaze shifted sharply to the crystal ball like I'd just seen something real interesting in it. "I can offer you a choice of the cards or the crystal ball, or I can deal directly with your palm. Put up or shut up."

Curiosity overcame Letty. "Oh, well, Maisie, I suppose we ought to let her try. You better sit down and have a reading."

"Why me?" said Maisie.

"Because I say so," Letty replied.

Maisie flopped into the chair, which threatened to collapse under her. I made an interesting pattern with my cards.

"Cross my palm with silver," I told her.

"What?"

"Gimme a nickel, Maisie," I explained.

Maisie whimpered. She had nothing but the coins on her costume. But Letty was quick to fish a nickel out of her Theda Bara outfit. Letty probably figured I was going to scare Maisie out of her wits and ruin her digestion. She wanted to see how I'd do it. I decided to use Maisie for bait.

Slipping the nickel into one of my pockets, I reached for her hand. It was somewhat sticky and smelled strongly of licorice.

"Hmmmmm." I stared deeply into her palm, which was all hills and no valleys. Her Lifeline looked like a Parker House roll.

"That's real interesting, that is," I murmured. She tried to pull her hand away, but I had a good grip on it.

"See that little bitty line branching off there?" I asked, pointing at nothing. Maisie scanned her own palm. "That's your travel line. You will make no great journeys in your life, neither over land nor sea. You will look upon no foreign shores."

Above us Letty made an impatient sound, but Maisie was falling under my spell.

"And see that line right there?" I pointed at smooth pink flesh. "That's your romantic life. Would you look at the size of that thing!"

"Where?" said Maisie. The coins on her forehead jangled. Letty edged nearer.

"Oh, yeah, romance with a capital *R* is heading your way. It will sweep you off your feet. Better yet, it will last. I see four children in here, maybe six."

Maisie was staring holes into her own hand. "Six!" she breathed. Letty was peering baldly over Maisie's big bejeweled shoulder now.

"Who is my great love to be, Blossom?" She was quivering like jelly.

She had me there. I couldn't imagine. I thought of giving her Champ Ferguson or even Bub Timmons. But then I thought: *Oh, well, shoot, why get her hopes up?*

"My vision grows dim," I moaned, letting my eyes roll halfway back into my head. "Your palm is an open book to me, but the print is fine and growing faint." I let my head loll, but by now Maisie had a grip on my hand and was hanging on for dear life.

"Your great love is a mystery man who will reveal his identity to you and you alone. All I can make out is that he's a tall, thin fellow who—ah—likes big women."

"That's me," Maisie whispered, wringing my hand.

It was not my best work, but it did a job on Maisie. I blinked and sat up straight. "What did I say? Where am I? What time is it?"

Maisie slumped in a daze before me, staring off into space.

Letty fished up another nickel and slapped it on

the table. "Me next," she said, elbowing Maisie out of the customer's chair. I fanned the deck on the table.

"Take a card, Letty. Any card."

*

While she was making her selection, I thought of what I knew of Letty's fate. Recalling the future, I saw Letty's granddaughter-to-be. I looked ahead seventy Halloweens and saw Heather, the spitting image of Letty. I saw Heather running her own little gang of girls at Bluffleigh Heights Magnet Middle School.

I foresaw Letty herself living to a ripe old age down in . . . Sun City, Arizona. Probably in the lap of luxury if I know Letty. I needed no crystal ball or deck of cards or palm for her.

But still, I pondered.

She turned up the four of diamonds, which is not an interesting card in itself.

"Hmmmmm, that's real interesting, that is."

"Quit stalling," Letty snapped, fiddling with her mantilla.

"Draw another card," I said, playing for time.

She twitched over the ace of spades.

"Whoops!" I jerked back and slapped my forehead. Letty flinched, too, and Maisie, looming over us, let out a little yelp.

"Can't be," I gasped. "Draw one more time. You owe it to yourself."

Her hand quivered as she turned up another ace

of spades. No wonder this is Mama's favorite deck.

Letty grabbed her throat, and Maisie grabbed her chins. I let my eyes roll all the way back. But I came to myself at once. Under all her white powder Letty's face had gone whiter. I swept up the three cards, reshuffled the deck, and slipped it into one of my pockets.

Fishing up a nickel, I flipped it on the table. "This here reading is at an end," I explained. "You can have your nickel back, Letty."

She took back her nickel quick enough. But her little black rosebud mouth trembled. "You better tell me, Blossom," she said in a tiny, tragic voice. "I better know what those cards are saying."

"Yes, she better know," said Maisie.

"Nobody thanks the bearer of bad news," I remarked. "Besides, I could be wrong. Possibly."

"Oh, I doubt it," Maisie blurted. "You were right on the button with me."

"Give me a hint anyhow," Letty said, twitching.

"I can't take the responsibility," I said. "I'll just have a squint at the crystal ball to double-check."

"Do that," Maisie urged.

I made a couple passes over the crystal ball. The flame from the candle reflected on the smooth glass. Back went my eyeballs till I was showing all white and seeing nothing.

"I see a peaceful scene and hear harps," I moaned mournfully.

"Oh, heaven help us," Maisie murmured. Letty was speechless.

"I see a group gathered around an open grave. Oh, how they're weeping and carrying on! But the floral tributes are lovely."

Maisie whimpered, but Letty wasn't breathing.

"Too soon, too soon," I lamented. "It's the grave of a young girl cut off in her prime or possibly sooner. A young *unmarried* girl, prominent in this community.

"My vision grows dim," I continued. "I can read this ball like a book; but it's clouding over, and we're spared from knowing the name of this deceased young . . . spinster."

My chin fell on my chest, but I jerked upright at once. "What did I say? Where am I? What time is it?"

But Letty was already at the door, and Maisie was struggling to keep her on her feet. "*She's a liar,*" Letty shrieked, throwing her arms around and grabbing air. "*It's a well-known fact. Ask anybody.*"

"Well, all I know is," Maisie said, "she was right on the button with me."

Cleopatra and Theda Bara went off down the stairs scared silly, which is about as good an advertisement for my business as I could get.

Before that Halloween night was over, I had customers waiting in line. I was passing out fortunes left and right and getting real good. I nearly worked the spots off Mama's cards, and my pockets bulged with nickels.

You can't go far wrong by giving the public what it wants and throwing in the occasional thrill.

19

It was near the witching hour of midnight before an important customer entered the Gypsy's tent and fell under my power.

Various teachers had dropped in through the evening to support our fund raiser and to keep an eye on us. Even Miss Blankenship had turned out. It was reported that she approved of the sign from *Hamlet* over our front door. But she hadn't come up to have her fortune told. Anybody as near retirement as Miss Blankenship isn't looking to the future.

But lo and behold, Mr. Lacy, the history teacher, as the official chaperon for this Haunted House, called on me. Clinging to his arm was none other than Miss Fuller of Girls' Gym.

"Better yet," I muttered, seemingly to myself, when I caught sight of her.

Miss Fuller was dolled up in a medley of flowing scarves. Her hair was swept up artistically above a colorful bandeau. Though her eyes are ever sad, they were bright tonight. She was riveted to Mr. Lacy's side.

He was in one of his natty outfits with matching haberdashery. "Well, Blossom," he boomed in his teacherish voice, "they tell me you have turned out to be the star attraction!"

He hovered there in the door with Miss Fuller hanging on him like a drowning woman.

"I hope you are a better student of the future than you are in my history class. Ha-ha."

"Oh, Ambrose," Miss Fuller simpered, "you are such a card."

I scooted my crystal ball into place.

"Good evening, folks," I said. "Step right in. Who's first?"

"Oh, ha-ha," booms Mr. Lacy. "I don't think Miss Fuller and I are in the market for any fortunes this evening. We have just stopped by to wish you well."

"Many thanks," I said, arranging my shawl, "but this is a place of business, and there are others waiting."

"Oh, Ambrose," says Miss Fuller, bending his sleeve, "go on and have a reading. These children need encouragement."

"Anything you say," he replied, giving her the old eye. Then he marched over to me, smirking.

"Take a chair," I told him. "You'll need it."

Smirking still, Mr. Lacy laid out his large white hand on the table. "I hear you are first-rate with palms," he boomed encouragingly.

"I'll just take a peek into the crystal ball if it's all

the same to you," I said. The candle was burning low now, and I'd counted on that.

Miss Fuller crept up behind where Mr. Lacy sat. Now she was looking fondly down at him. I rolled my eyeballs abruptly back, and both my customers started.

A breeze seemed to stir the sheets of the tent that enclosed us. The wavering candle threw long shadows. "Oh, my," Miss Fuller murmured.

I made a couple passes over the crystal ball, seeming to read it with the whites of my eyes.

"I don't think that can be good for her vision," Miss Fuller said.

"Hush, honey," Mr. Lacy replied.

I made a couple more passes over the crystal ball. "That's real interesting," I remarked, "but strange." My hands cupped my face, and I swayed from side to side.

"I wish she'd quit doing that with her eyes," Miss Fuller whispered.

My knee knocked the underside of the table, and the crystal ball jiggled, taking on a little life of its own.

Then I rolled my eyes back to a seeing position. A worried look crossed my face. "What we have here is an unusual situation," I explained to Mr. Lacy. "You don't seem to have any future at all to speak of."

"Oh, ha-ha," he boomed uncertainly. He began to rise. He wouldn't have minded leaving right then.

"Never mind, Blossom," Miss Fuller said kindly. "As I've often said in the locker room, you can't win them all."

"But poor student of history that I am," I continued, "I believe I'll try to delve around in your past, Mr. Lacy."

"Oh, a little personal history?" He smirked again, broader than before.

"You got it," I said. "After all, what is history but mankind's record where we look for guidance? We search the past for wisdom because the future is the Great Unknown!"

"I couldn't have put it better myself," Mr. Lacy said. The last of the candlelight gleamed in his yellow wavy hair.

"Here it comes," I said, peering deep into the blank ball. "Here comes Wisdom sharp and clear. Lay it on me!"

Fresh breezes seemed to whip the sheets around us. The screams of sophomores going through the deadman's dungeon far below our feet echoed upward.

"I see a small town, somewhat backward," I moaned distantly, "on the banks of the Mississippi River. I see steamboats drawn up to the wharf, taking on cotton and grain."

"How interesting," Miss Fuller remarked. Mr. Lacy said nothing.

"From the general condition of the place," I moaned on, "I'd put us back about 1905, or 1906 at the latest."

Mr. Lacy stirred.

"I see a festive occasion and half the town turned out for the event." My nose was practically flat against the ball by now. "A wedding!" I exclaimed. "They're throwing rice at a happy couple."

"How sweet," Miss Fuller said.

"The bride is not much to look at," I observed, "but the groom is one good-looking dude."

Mr. Lacy's white hand stole up to smooth his yellow hair.

I fell back in the chair. "My vision grows dim, dim," I nearly sobbed. "Dark clouds obscure this joyous scene.

"But hark!" Back my nose went to the ball. I was reading it like a book, and you could have heard a pin drop. "The groom is a husband now, and a bad one. I see the bride, now a wife, weeping in despair. She has been deceived and knows it!"

"For shame," Miss Fuller said.

"This poor deceived wife is tearing her hair and . . . rocking a cradle!"

"A *cradle*?" Miss Fuller plucked nervously at her drapings.

As if by chance, the fringe on my shawl swept over the candle, snuffing it out. We were in darkness now, within the swaying sheets.

"I can almost hear this abandoned wife and mother's voice," I said in rather a loud tone.

Silence fell.

I spoke again, louder. *"I say I can almost hear this abandoned wife and mother's voice."*

In a far corner of the darkened room something moved behind the sheets. It was only a shadow at first. Then there was the tiniest pinpoint of light, floating like a firefly.

"*Owwww*" came the weirdest voice you ever heard. Miss Fuller had Mr. Lacy in a hammerlock. Nobody breathed.

"*Owwww, Ambrose! Ambrose!*" The sheets stirred, and the pinpoint of lamplight grew to a glow. "*Wherefore art thou, Ambrose?*"

A lamp was held up by a bony hand. Its pale light filtering through the sheet fell on the frozen faces of Miss Fuller and Mr. Lacy. They stared in horror, and I had the willies myself.

There was only the hint of a wan and mournful face behind the sheet, for all the world like an abandoned wife and mother.

"*Owwww, Ambrose,*" the thing said, "*it's me, yore lovin' wife. Why have you run off and left me, Ambrose? Don't you know me, sweetheart? It's me . . . Blanche!*"

Mr. Lacy started from his chair. "Son of a—"

"Who?" Miss Fuller asked. "Who's Blanche?"

The thing went right on talking. "*And here beside me, Ambrose, is yore lovin' little child.*"

There was a short struggle behind the sheet. Another ghostly form, much smaller, was dragged up to our attention. "*Here is yore little boy. Wave to Papa . . . Leonard.*"

Mr. Lacy crashed back in his chair.

"Leonard?" Miss Fuller asked. "Who's Leonard?"

A bony hand reached up to turn the lamp down. It gleamed like a firefly floating and went out. The pair of ghostly figures, the big one and the little one, faded.

Then things went haywire.

We remained in dark silence for an instant. Then Mr. Lacy lunged my way. He fumbled for the crystal ball and grabbed it. Then he hauled off and heaved it toward the sheet. It exploded against the far wall with a deafening sound. Miss Fuller commenced screaming and wouldn't stop.

20

THE WITCHING HOUR HAD PASSED, and November was upon us. There was already gray dawn light in the east, and the old Leverette farmhouse was abandoned once more.

The last of our customers had departed, and the Shambaughs' Packard had long since called for Letty and her club. I had no doubt they were all snug in warm beds by now.

Still, I lingered in the upstairs room. I'd folded up all the sheets of my tent and pulled down my Madame Blossom Tells All sign. Now I was sweeping up the crystal ball that had shattered all over the room. Somehow, I wanted to leave the room neat for Jeremy-to-be.

Though I figured I was alone with my thoughts, I heard a footstep at the door, crunching on broken glass. I turned to see a shadow on the threshold. It moved and was Alexander.

He hesitated, still suspicious of this particular room.

"Blossom, you still here?"

"If I'm not, Alexander, you're looking at my ghost."

He peered from side to side. "Don't talk that way," he muttered. "I heard sweeping, so I figured you hadn't gone." He stepped cautiously into the room, carrying a couple of punch cups. "I was cleaning up the monster's kitchen and thought maybe you'd like a cup of grape juice. After all, you put in a pretty good night's work, I have to admit."

"Many thanks, Alexander." I propped the broom against the wall, and we settled at my table. It seemed empty without the crystal ball. Alexander placed a punch cup before me and withdrew his hand, fast.

"Don't worry," I said. "I've told enough fortunes for one night."

Alexander nodded. "That's what everybody says. You outdid yourself with Mr. Lacy. He took off like a bat out of you-know-where. Miss Fuller was right at his heels. She was screaming to beat the band and wouldn't stop."

"He was nothing but a philandering married man," I remarked wearily, "and he was sparking both Miss Fuller and Miss Spaulding. If he wants to save his worthless hide, he'll be on the milk train out of Bluff City this very morning."

Alexander considered this. "I hope they'll be in no hurry to find a new history teacher," he said, which is the way a boy thinks.

We sipped a little grape juice, and then he said, "Blossom, how did you get the goods on Mr. Lacy?

Did you use the crystal ball on him, or did you go off into one of your spells?"

I twitched my elbows slightly. "Well, now, Alexander, that's an interesting point. As you know, I have a number of Powers to draw on. And as I've often said, a Gift is a curse unless you put it to work. Now you take, for example, a deck of cards. I've done some of my best work this very evening with this very deck."

Reaching into a pocket, I withdrew the cards and fanned them on the table before us.

The room had gone from black to gray. In the cold light of dawn they were only ordinary playing cards, greasy from Mama's hand.

Alexander waited, almost politely, for whatever tall tale I cared to think up.

But Halloween was over, and it was just me and Alexander Armsworth there together. So I told him the truth.

I told him it was Mama who'd known about Mr. Lacy's shameful past. Naturally that brought in Daisy-Rae and Roderick, whom Alexander had already more or less met. I had to work them into this conversation, for Daisy-Rae played the role of Blanche, Mr. Lacy's poor, deceived wife. And Roderick played the role of his abandoned little son, Leonard.

It was lucky indeed that Mr. Lacy hadn't knocked one or both of them senseless when he let fly with that crystal ball. Even that polecat's aim was bad.

Of course, in the confusion that followed, Daisy-Rae and Roderick had slipped off to their chicken coop home and were doubtless fast asleep by now.

Alexander rubbed his chin for all the world like Jeremy. "Blossom, do you mean to tell me that Daisy-Rae sleeps in a chicken coop all night and lives all day in the girls' rest room at Bluff City High School? Is that what you're telling me?"

The trouble with the truth is that it's hard to believe.

*

But by and by I got Alexander convinced. It was time we headed for home. The sun was all but up. Though I hadn't liked to leave this room, somehow I didn't mind with Alexander by my side.

We were climbing down the creaky stairs to the cobwebby hall. "Now that Daisy-Rae has helped out at our Haunted House fund raiser," I said, "I think I can convince her to be a regular freshman. A little nudge or two, and I'll have her attending classes."

Alexander nodded his approval of this plan.

"If Daisy-Rae's going to be a real freshman," I observed, "she'll naturally need a beanie. But I'll find one for her somewheres."

Alexander reached up to his bare head. "I've lost my beanie," he said, "somewheres."

"Is that a fact," I remarked, and he gave me one of his most suspicious looks.

His suspicions deepened when I led him to the

dining room. It was bare in there except for some burned-out jack-o'-lanterns and the old gasolier fixture hanging down. The china closet door stood open.

He saw that Roderick was not lurking inside, ready to scare him out of a year's growth again. Still, he was puzzled when I said, "I'd be obliged if you'd check around in that china closet for a loose floorboard."

He went down on all fours and peered inside. "All the floorboards are loose," he said in a hollow voice.

I reached into one of my many pockets and fished up the spelling medal. "Just hide this medal of mine under one of them boards."

When he'd wedged it tight under the floor, he sat back on his heels. "How come we're burying your medal, Blossom?"

"I've left it as a token of friendship," I told him, "for a kid of my acquaintance."

"A boy?" Alexander wondered.

I nodded.

"Is it anybody I know? It's not Champ, is it? Or Bub?"

"Mercy, no, Alexander." I shook my head till the hoops swung in my ears. "It's a boy yet to be. He won't be born for many years."

Alexander rubbed his chin in thought. "And yet you know him, Blossom."

I nodded.

"There are more things in heaven and earth,
    Alexander,
    Than are dreamt of in your philosophy."

"*Hamlet*?" he inquired.

"Act One," I answered.

Then me and Alexander Armsworth walked out into the bright November morning, almost hand in hand.

ABOUT THE AUTHOR

Richard Peck attended Oxford University in England and holds degrees from DePauw University and Southern Illinois University.

He has written two other books about Blossom Culp and Alexander Armsworth: *The Ghost Belonged to Me*, which was an ALA Notable Book, and *Ghosts I Have Been*, which was selected a Best Book for Young Adults by the American Library Association. The Bluff City in these books and in *The Dreadful Future of Blossom Culp* is Richard Peck's view of his own hometown, Decatur, Illinois, as it was many years ago.

Mr. Peck's most recent books for Delacorte were *Secrets of the Shopping Mall* and *Close Enough to Touch*, which was also an ALA Best Book for Young Adults. Mr. Peck lives in New York City and in a cabin on Candlewood Lake in Connecticut.